THIS DIARY BELONGS TO:

Nikki J. Maxwell

PRIVATE & CONFIDENTIAL

If found, please return to ME for REWARD!

(NO SNOOPING ALLOWED!! ☹)

Also by Rachel Renée Russell

Dork Diaries
Dork Diaries: Party Time

Coming Soon...
Dork Diaries: Pop Star

Rachel Renée Russell

Double
DORK
diaries

SIMON AND SCHUSTER

First published as an omnibus edition in Great Britain in 2011 by Simon and Schuster UK Ltd,
A CBS COMPANY
Simon & Schuster UK Ltd
1ˢᵗ Floor, 222 Gray's Inn Road, London WC1X 8HB

DORK DIARIES first published in Great Britain in 2010 by Simon and Schuster UK Ltd,
a CBS company. Originally published in 2009 in the USA by Aladdin, an imprint of
Simon & Schuster Children's Publishing Division, 1230 Avenue of Americas, New York.

DORK DIARIES: PARTY TIME first published in Great Britain in 2010 by Simon and Schuster
UK Ltd, a CBS company. Originally published as DORK DIARIES: TALES FROM A NOT-SO-
POPULAR PARTY GIRL in 2010 in the USA by Aladdin, an imprint of Simon & Schuster
Children's Publishing Division, 1230 Avenue of Americas, New York.

Copyright Ó Rachel Renée Russell 2009 and 2010
Book design by Lisa Vega

The right of Rachel Renée Russell to be identified as the author and illustrator of this work has
been asserted by her in accordance with sections 77 and 78 of the
Copyright, Design and Patents Act, 1988.

A CIP catalogue record for this book is available from the British Library.

ISBN 978-0-85707-218-4

www.simonandschuster.co.uk
www.dorkdiaries.com

9 10 8

Printed and bound by CPI Group (UK) Ltd, Croydon, CR0 4YY

New school. New crush. New mean girl.
New diary, so Nikki can spill all about it.

Get ready to enter the disastrous life
of Nikki Maxwell in

Sometimes I wonder if my mom is BRAIN DEAD. Then there are days when I know she is.

Like today.

The drama started this morning when I casually asked if she would buy me one of those cool new iPhones that do almost everything. I considered it a necessity of life, second only to maybe oxygen.

What better way to clinch a spot in the CCP (Cute, Cool & Popular) group at my new private school, Westchester Country Day, than by dazzling them with a wicked new mobile phone.

Last year, it seemed like I was the ONLY student in my ENTIRE middle school who didn't have one ☹. So I bought an older, used phone super-cheap on eBay.

It was bigger than what I wanted, but I figured I couldn't go wrong for the clearance price of only $12.99.

I put my phone in my locker and spread the word that everyone could now call me with all the JUICY gossip on my NEW telephone! Then I counted down the minutes before my social life started heating up.

I got really nervous when two of the CCP girls came walking down the hall in my direction chatting on their mobile phones.

←ME

They came right over to my locker and started acting super-friendly. Then they invited me to sit with them at lunch and I was like, "Umm . . . okay." But deep down inside I was jumping up and down and doing my Snoopy "happy dance".

Then things got really strange. They said they had heard about my new $600 Juicy Couture designer mobile phone and that everyone (meaning the rest of the CCP crew) couldn't wait to see it.

I was about to explain that I had said, "juicy gossip on my _new_ phone" NOT, "_new_ gossip on my _Juicy_ phone", but I never got a chance because, unfortunately, my telephone starting ringing. Very abnormally loudly. I was trying my best to ignore it,

but both of the CCP girls were staring at me like, "Well, aren't you going to answer it?!"

Obviously, I didn't want to answer it because I had a really bad feeling they were going to be a little disappointed when they actually saw my phone.

So I just stood there praying that it would stop ringing, but it didn't. And pretty soon everyone in the hallway was staring at me too.

Finally, I gave in, snatched open my locker and answered the phone. Mainly to stop that AWFUL ringing.

I was like, "Hello? Umm . . . sorry. Wrong number."

And when I turned around, both of the CCP girls were running down the hall screaming, "Make it go away! Make it go away!" I guessed it probably meant they DIDN'T want me to sit with them at lunch anymore, which really sucked.

The most important lesson I learned last year was that having a CRUDDY phone — or NONE at all — can totally RUIN your social life. While hordes of celebrity party girls regularly FORGET to wear undies, not a single one would be caught dead without her mobile phone. Which was why I was nagging my mom about buying me an iPhone.

I've tried saving up my own money to buy one, but it was impossible to do. Mainly because I'm an artist and TOTALLY ADDICTED to drawing!

4

Like, if I don't do it every day, I'll go NUTZ!

I spend ALL of my cash on sketchbooks, pencils, pens, art camp and other stuff. Hey, I'm so BROKE, I have a milkshake on layaway at McDonald's!

Anyway, when mom came home from the mall with a special back-to-school present for me I was pretty sure I knew what it was.

She rambled on and on about how my attending a new private school was going to be a "stressful time of tremendous personal growth" and how my best "coping mechanism" would be to "communicate" my "thoughts and feelings".

I was absolutely ECSTATIC

because you can communicate with a

NEW PHONE!

Right?! ☺

I kind of zoned out on most of what my mom was

5

saying because I was DAYDREAMING about all of the cool ring tones, music and movies I was going to download. It was going to be LOVE AT FIRST SIGHT!

But after my mom *finally* finished her little speech, she smiled really big, hugged me and handed me a BOOK.

I opened it and FRANTICALLY flipped through the pages, figuring that maybe she had hidden my new phone inside.

It made perfect sense at the time because all the advertisements said it was *the* thinnest model on the market.

But slowly it dawned on me that my mom had NOT got me a phone and my so-called present was just a stupid little book! ☹

Talk about major HEARTBREAK!

Then I noticed that ALL the pages of the book were BLANK.

I was like, OH. NO. SHE. DIDN'T!

My mom had given me two things: a DIARY and irrefutable evidence she IS, in fact,

CLINICALLY BRAIN DEAD!!

Absolutely no one writes their most intimate feelings and deep, dark secrets in a diary anymore! WHY?!

Because just one or two people knowing all your BIZ could completely ruin your reputation.

You're supposed to post this kind of juicy stuff online in your BLOG so MILLIONS can read it!!!

Only a TOTAL DORK would be caught WRITING in a DIARY!!

This is THE worst present I have ever received in my entire life! I wanted to yell at the top of my lungs:

"Mom, I don't need a STUPID book with 288

BLANK
pages!!"

What I NEED is to be able to "communicate" my "thoughts and feelings" to my friends using my very own mobile phone.

Wait! Silly me. I keep forgetting. I don't have any friends. YET. But that could change overnight and I need to be prepared. With a shiny, new phone!

In the meantime I will NOT write in this diary again.

NEVER! EVER!!

Okay. I know I said I'd never write in this diary again. I meant it at the time. I'm definitely not the kind of girl who curls up with a diary and a box of Godiva chocolates to write a bunch of really sappy stuff about my dreamy boyfriend, my first kiss or my overwhelming ANGST about the HORRIFIC discovery that I'm a PRINCESS of a small French-speaking principality and now worth MILLIONS.

THIS IS SO <u>NOT</u> ME!

Pedicure

Designer Clothing

Beauty

Brains

Perfect Skin

Shiny Hair

Cute, flirty habit of twirling hair that drives the guys wild!

Manicure

Chocolates (from adoring boyfriend)

Perfect Body

Exciting Diary

Princess Tiara

MY LIFE TOTALLY SUCKS!!

All day I wandered around my new school like a zombie in lip gloss. Not a single person bothered to say hi.

THIS IS ME!

MOST OF THE TIME I FEEL INVISIBLE!

How am I supposed to fit in at a snobby prep school like Westchester Country Day?! This place has a Starbucks in the cafeteria!

I wish my dad had NEVER been awarded a bug extermination contract from this school.

They can take their little pity scholarship and give it to someone who wants and needs it, because I sure DON'T!

It's way past midnight and I'm about to freak out because I still don't have my homework done. The assignment is for Honours English Lit and we're reading *A Midsummer Night's Dream* by Shakespeare. I was kind of surprised, because I didn't know he wrote teen chick lit.

It's about a mischievous fairy named Puck who tries to break up a really cute couple lost in an enchanted forest.

Then, this guy with a donkey head crashes a big, fairy party and hooks up with their queen. Pretty weird stuff!

Our homework assignment is to complete three essay questions about PUCK:

1. Would you consider Puck the protagonist of the play? Why or why not?

2. How do Puck's personality and actions set the mood of the play?

3. Use your imagination and provide either a detailed physical description or a drawing of Puck.

The first two questions weren't that hard, and I finished them in no time at all. However, the third question threw me for a loop.

I didn't have the slightest idea what Puck looked like.

But I tried to imagine him with cute little pointy ears and AS HOT AS :

NICK JONAS ➚

CORBIN BLEU   JUSTIN TIMBERLAKE

I was also dying to know if having a messed-up name like Puck had completely RUINED his life.

I bet the popular kids at his school called him "Puke", "Schmuck", "Yuck", or something worse.

POOR PUCK ☹!!

I tried to go to that educational website "Wiki-something-or-other" that everyone plagiarises to find a picture of Puck.

But I couldn't remember the name of it and was too lazy to Google it.

I was really surprised to hear a knock on my bedroom door this late at night and I assumed it was my six-year-old sister, Brianna.

About a week ago she lost one of her front teeth and buried it in the backyard to see if it would grow. She is FOREVER doing crazy-weird stuff like that.

My mom says it's because she's still a little kid. But I personally think it's because she has the IQ of a box of crayons.

As a little joke I told Brianna the tooth fairy collected teeth from children all over the world and then Super Glued them together to make dentures for old people.

I explained that she was in BIG TROUBLE with the tooth fairy, seeing as she had dug a hole and buried her tooth somewhere out in the backyard.

The funniest part was that Brianna TOTALLY believed me. She actually dug up half of Mom's flower garden trying to find her tooth.

Since then Brianna has been paranoid that the tooth fairy is going to sneak into her room in the middle of the night and pull out ALL her teeth to make dentures.

But my prank kind of backfired, because now she absolutely REFUSES to use the bathroom at night unless I first check to make sure the tooth fairy is not hiding behind the shower curtain or under the bath towels.

And if I'm not quick enough Brianna will have a little "accident" right on my bedroom carpet.

MY LITTLE SISTER, BRIANNA

B-BUT, WHAT IF THE **TOOTH FAIRY** IS HIDING IN THERE?! **OOPS...!!**

ACCIDENT! ☹

Unfortunately, I had to learn the hard way that (contrary to the TV commercial) Carpet Fresh DOES NOT remove all odours.

Lucky for me it wasn't Brianna at my door, but my parents.

MOM

DAD

Before I could say, "Come in", they just kind of barged in, like they always do, which really irritated me, because this is *supposed* to be MY room! And as an American citizen, I have a constitutional right to PRIVACY which they keep invading.

The next time my parents and Brianna come rollin' up in here, I'm gonna scream:

"Hey! Why don't y'all just MOVE IN?!"

Anyway, my parents said they were surprised to see that I was still up doing homework and they wanted to know how things were going at school.

It was really strange, because just as I was about to answer, I had a total meltdown right on the spot and burst into tears.

My parents were shocked and stared at me and then at each other. Finally, Mom hugged me and said, "My poor little Boo-Boo!" which only made me feel WORSE.

Not fitting in at school was bad enough. But now I had to suffer the additional humiliation of being the only fourteen-year-old *still* being called "little Boo-Boo"! Suddenly my dad's face lit up.

"Hey, I've got a great idea! We know you've been under a lot of stress lately with our move and your new school. I bet if we posted some positive affirmations all around the house, it would help you adjust. You think?"

I was like, "Okay, Dad, THIS is what I think: It's a STUPID idea! Like sticky notes with corny sayings on them will solve my problem of being a TOTAL

LOSER at school. You wanna know what else I think? The article I read about bug extermination chemicals killing off brain cells is probably true!"

But I just said it inside my head, so no one heard it but me.

My parents kept staring at me and it was starting to creep me out. Finally, after what seemed like forever, my mom smiled and said, "Honey, just remember, we love you! And if you need us, we're right down the hall."

They walked back to their bedroom and for several minutes I could hear their muffled voices. I guessed that they were probably discussing whether or not I should be committed to a mental hospital right then or first thing in the morning.

Since it was so late I decided to finish my Puck assignment during study hall.

I wonder if you still have to hand in homework when you're locked up in a PSYCHO WARD?

My new issue of *That's So Hot!* magazine says the secret to happiness is the four Fs:

Friends, Fun, Fashion & Flirting

But, unfortunately, the closest I've ever got to "friends, fun, fashion and flirting" is having a locker right next to MacKenzie Hollister.

She's THE most popular girl in the eighth grade.

Lucky me! ☹

I had just finished fighting my way through the crowded hallways to get to my locker and had almost been trampled alive.

Then, suddenly, as if by magic, the huge mob of students parted right down the centre, just like the Red Sea.

That's when I first saw MacKenzie strutting down

the hallway like it was the runway of a Paris fashion show or something.

She had blonde hair and blue eyes and was dressed like she had just left a photo shoot for the cover of *Teen Vogue.*

And everyone (except me) immediately fell under her powerful hypnotic spell and totally lost their minds.

"What's up, MacKenzie!"

"You look hot, MacKenzie!"

"Are you coming to my party this weekend, MacKenzie?"

"Love your shoes, MacKenzie!"

"Will you marry me, MacKenzie?"

"You'll NEVER guess who has a crush on you, MacKenzie!"

"Is that *another* designer purse, MacKenzie?"

"Fabulous hair today, MacKenzie!"

"I'll pluck out my eye with a pencil and eat it with a Spam and mustard sandwich IF ONLY you'll sit with me at lunch today, MacKenzie!"

Which also proves my theory that there's ALWAYS at least ONE seriously mentally ill WEIRDO in EVERY middle school across America!

It was "MacKenzie! MacKenzie! MacKenzie!" When she walked up to the locker right next to mine, I knew then and there I was going to have a VERY bad school year.

Being so close to the radiance of her awesome yet sickening perfection just made me feel like a humongous LOSER. And it didn't help that she was HOGGING most of my personal space ☹!!

Hey, it wasn't like I was jealous of her or anything. I mean, how totally juvenile would THAT be?!

Between classes MacKenzie and her friends are

forever standing right in front of MY locker, "GGG-ing."

That means:

GIGGLING, GOSSIPING AND GLOSSING

And whenever I get up the nerve to say, "Excuse me, but I really need to get into my locker," she just ignores me or rolls her eyes and says stuff like, "Annoying much?" or "What's HER problem?"

And I'm like, "Hey, girlfriend! I don't have no STINKIN' problem!"

But I just say it inside my head, so no one really hears it except me.

However, deep down I'm troubled and ashamed that a tiny part of me - a very dark and primitive side - would totally LOVE to be best friends with MacKenzie!

26

And I find that part of myself SO disgusting . . . I
could . . . VOMIT!

But on a much happier note I'm really into lip gloss
too.

My favorite one right now is Krazy Kissalicious
Strawberry Crush Glitterati.

It's yummy and tastes just like strawberry
cheesecake.

Unfortunately, no supercute hunk (like Brandon
Roberts, the guy who sits in front of me in my
biology class) has developed a huge crush on me and
fallen in love with my fabulous glossy lips, like in
all of those KRAZY KISSALICIOUS television
commercials.

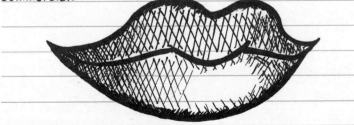

But, hey! It could happen!

In the meantime I've decided to try and enjoy my single status.

Oh, I almost forgot! Dad is supposed to pick me up after school today to take me to my dentist appointment.

PLEASE, PLEASE, PLEASE don't let him pick me up in his work van with the five-foot-long plastic roach on top.

I would absolutely DIE if anyone found out I only attend this school due to his bug extermination contract!

☹!!

MacKenzie and her snobby friends are about to get on my last nerve! They're always making NASTY comments about any girl who wanders within six feet of them. I mean who do they think they are?

THE FASHION POLICE?!

"HI, SWEETIE! YOU'RE UNDER ARREST FOR A FELONY FASHION VIOLATION!"

Today, in under one minute, MacKenzie gave out the following scathing fashion commentary while applying her lip gloss:

"Don't you need a LICENCE to be that UGLY?"

"That outfit would be perfect for Goodwill. If she knows what's GOOD for her, she WILL burn it."

"OMG! I bought that exact same sweater she's wearing! For my dog, from PetSmart."

"What's that awful STANK?! She's supposed to spray on the perfume, not marinate in it."

"She has SO much acne, she uses a special makeup brand. It's called Why Bother."

"What's up with her new hairstyle? It looks like a small mammal made a nest in her hair, had babies and died!"

"She thinks she's SO cute. She's just living proof that manure can actually grow legs and walk."

To call MacKenzie a "mean girl" would be an understatement. She's VICIOUS! She's a PIT BULL in glittery eye shadow and Jimmy Choo flip-flops!

I think I've finally figured out why I don't fit in at this school. I need a new designer wardrobe from one of those really expensive teen shops at the mall.

You know, the ones where the salesgirls dress like Hannah Montana and have pierced belly buttons, blonde highlights and phony smiles.

But what drives me INSANE is their nasty habit of unexpectedly snatching open the curtain of your dressing room and popping their head inside when you're, like, HALF NAKED. It's enough to make you want to slap those blonde highlights right out of their hair.

And when you look in the mirror you can obviously see that the outfit looks HORRIBLE on you. But those salesgirls just smile really big and act cute and perky and LIE TO YOUR FACE by saying the outfit (1) looks totally fabulous, (2) brings out your natural skin tones and (3) complements your eye colour.

They'll tell you this EVEN if you're trying on one of those huge green lawn-size HEFTY TRASH BAGS!

"HON! THAT LOOKS SO-0-0-0-0 CUTE ON YOU!"

ME (WEARING A TRASH BAG)

I also HATE clothes that are "SNOBBY CHIC."

It's when the exact same outfit looks TOTALLY different on two very similar girls. The more popular you are at school, the BETTER it looks on you, and the more unpopular you are, the WORSE it looks on you. I can't tell you HOW a snobby chic outfit mysteriously knows all of this personal stuff about you, but it obviously DOES!

WHY I HATE SNOBBY CHIC FASHIONS!

The SNOBBY CHIC phenomenon is quite a mind-boggling thing. Hopefully, Congress will allocate funding for scientists to study it, along with how socks mysteriously disappear from the dryer. But, until then, BUYER BEWARE ☹!

Anyway, after my mom buys me a designer wardrobe, I'm going to walk right up to MacKenzie and her little entourage and tell them off really good.

But before I say anything I'm going to put my hands on my hips and do that neck-roll thing like Tyra Banks, just to show them how much attitude I really have.

Tyra says every girl must find her own inner beauty deep down inside and ignore all the HATERS. She's SO sweet and a wonderful role model!

Although, I have to admit, she's kind of SCARY on *America's Next Top Model*.

Especially when she's screaming stuff at those poor contestants like, "You FAT, worthless SKANKS! You will NEVER, EVER make it in the modelling industry like I did! You have NO idea how much I've BLED and SUFFERED! And wipe that SMIRK off yo' face before I SLAP it off, you little #@$%&!"

Then she starts crying hysterically and popping Tic Tac breath mints.

I just LOVE that girl!

I've decided that I'm going to tell MacKenzie right to her face (on, like, maybe the last day of school) that just because she and her clones dress like

FASHIONISTAS,

they do NOT have the right to say really mean things about other people.

"People" being the girls whose moms make them shop at JCPenney, Sears, Target and Wal-Mart.

Girls like . . . well, ME!

Okay. It's NOT a big secret that the clothes from those stores AREN'T as hot as the clothes from the mall.

And yes, it's a huge inconvenience (and a definite

turnoff) to have to walk through the "OLD Ladies", "FAT Ladies" and "PREGNANT Ladies" departments to get to the one for "TEENS"...

No wonder most girls prefer those fancy teen shops in the mall!

FINDING THE TEEN DEPARTMENT

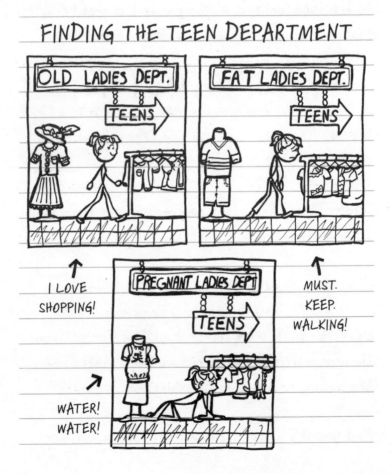

My mom says it really doesn't matter where your clothes come from as long as they're clean. Right?

WRONG!!

I wish I had a dollar for every time I've heard MacKenzie shriek, "OMG! WHERE are these PATHETIC girls buying such HIDEOUS clothes?! I'd come to school butt naked before I would EVER buy my fashions from a store that sells LAWN MOWERS!"

To be honest, I didn't know the stores I shopped at sold lawn mowers. And even if they do, big, fat, hairy deal.

It's not like the clothes smell like a lawn mower or something. At least, I hadn't noticed it.

The next time I go shopping I'm going to sniff the clothing before I buy anything, just to make sure.

I'm also going to wear a hat, wig, sunglasses and phony moustache so no one will recognise me.

WHATEVER!!

My mom and dad are driving me NUTS! In the past 72 hours they have posted all over the house 139 positive affirmations on rainbow-coloured sticky notes that say really stupid things like:

> "Be your OWN best friend. Invite YOURSELF over for a sleepover!"

Unfortunately, I never got a chance to read the one they stuck in the toaster slot thingy because it caught on fire when I tried to make a strawberry Pop-Tart for breakfast.

I had to dump my glass of orange juice on the sticky note to put it out.

And after that the toaster started melting, shooting blue electrical sparks and making a loud, angry noise like:

GRRRRRRAAAAAAAGGGG!!

I'm thinking we're probably going to need a new one.

But, what was really SCARY was that our house could have actually burnt to the ground. All because my parents stuck a sticky note in the toaster slot thingy.

I know my mom and dad mean well, but sometimes they're an

EMBARRASSMENT!

SUNDAY, SEPTEMBER 8

I'm already dreading that the weekend is almost
over and I have to go back to school tomorrow. It's
been one whole week and I still haven't made a single
friend. I've got this . . . OVERWHELMING . . .
sense of loneliness sitting in the pit of my stomach
like a . . . big, fat, poisonous . . . TOAD!

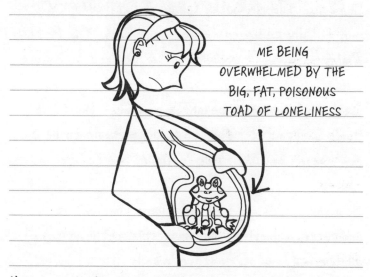

ME BEING
OVERWHELMED BY THE
BIG, FAT, POISONOUS
TOAD OF LONELINESS

I'm seriously thinking about asking my parents to let
me move back to the city and live with my grandma
so I can attend my old school.

I'll admit the school wasn't perfect. But I'd give

41

anything to hang out with my friends from art class again. I really, really miss them ☹!

Anyway, my grandma lives in one of those apartment buildings for elderly people "who are young at heart and committed to leading a full and active life". So she's up on ALL the latest fads and stuff.

She's also a little wacky (okay, A LOT WACKY) and totally addicted to the game show *The Price Is Right*.

Last year Grandma bought a computer from the Home Shopping Network to help her train to be a contestant on *The Price Is Right*.

Now she spends most of her spare time on her computer, memorising the suggested retail prices of all the major grocery store brands.

She plans to use all her research and game strategies to write a how-to manual called *The Price Is Right for Morons*.

Grandma says her book could be bigger than *Harry Potter*.

MY GRANDMA

I didn't think being on a game show took any special skills, but she told me you had to train like you would for the Super Bowl.

She took a few sips of her energy drink, stared at me real seriouslike and whispered, "Sweetie, when life presents challenges, you can be either a CHICKEN or a CHAMPION. The choice is YOURS!"

Then she started humming "Girls Just Want to Have Fun" really loudly.

43

I was like, JUST GREAT! Grandma is finally going SENILE! Doesn't she understand that some things in life you're STUCK with and powerless to change?! Jeez!

But I have to admit she has got pretty good at *The Price Is Right*. The last few times I saw her play along with the game show, she got every single price correct! It was amazing because she would have won, like, $549,321 in cash and prizes, including three cars, a boat, a trip for two to Niagara Falls and a lifetime supply of Depends adult diapers.

I gave her a big hug and said, "Grandma, you have mad skillz at the *Price Is Right* game and I'm really proud of you. But you should really try to get out of the house more often."

Grandma just smiled and said her life is exciting now that she's taking hip-hop dance lessons at the senior rec center. And her dance teacher, Krump Daddy, is "dope!"

Then she asked me if I wanted to see her "bust a move".

She was actually pretty good for a seventy-six-year-old! Grandma's a little WACKY, but you gotta LOVE her!

This morning the halls were plastered with colourful posters for Random Acts of Avant-Garde Art, our annual school art show.

I'm SUPER-excited because the first prize for each class is $500, cash! SWEET!

That would be enough for me to buy a mobile phone, a new outfit from the mall AND art supplies.

But most important, winning that award could transform me from a "socially challenged ART DORK" to a "socially charmed ART DIVA" practically overnight!

Who woulda thunk my art skillz could get me into the CCP clique?!

So I rushed down to the school office to get an entry form and was surprised to see a line had already formed.

And guess who else was there picking one up?

MacKenzie ☹!!!!

And as usual she was blabbering nonstop: "Like, since I'm going to be a model/fashion designer/pop star, I already have a portfolio of seven very HOT fashion illustrations for my FAB-4-EVER clothing line, which I also plan to wear on my very successful world tour as the opening act for Miley Cyrus, who of course will fall head over heels in love with MY designs and buy, like, a million dollars' worth. Then I'm going to enroll at a prestigious university like Harvard, Yale, or the Westchester Fashion Institute of Cosmetology, which, BTW, is owned by my aunt Clarissa!"

Okay. I'll admit I FREAKED OUT about having to compete against MacKenzie.

She just kept staring at me with her icy-blue eyes, and my stomach felt queasy and I got chill bumps.

Then, suddenly, I had an epiphany and I TOTALLY understood what my grandma meant when she said,

47

"You can be a CHICKEN
or a CHAMPION.
The choice is yours."

So I gathered all my strength and determination,
took a deep breath, and mustered the courage to
decide right there on the spot which one I was:

A BIG FAT CHICKEN!

When the office assistant asked
if I was there to pick up an entry
form for the avant-garde art
show, I just froze and started
clucking like a hen:

Buk, buk, buk-ka-a-ah!

Then, MacKenzie laughed, like ME
entering the competition was the
most ridiculous thing she had ever
heard.

That's when I spotted the yellow sign-up sheet for

library shelving assistants, also known as LSAs. Every day during study hall, a few kids get excused to go to the school library to shelve books. An LSA's life is about as exciting as watching paint dry.

So instead of trying to achieve my dream of winning a major art competition, I very STUPIDLY signed up to shelve DUSTY and BORING LIBRARY BOOKS!

MY FUTURE MISERABLE LIFE AS A LIBRARY SHELVING ASSISTANT

"IF I SEE ANOTHER BOOK, I'M GOING TO PUKE!"

And it's ALL MacKenzie's fault!! ☹

When I reported to the library during study hall, the librarian, Mrs Peach, gave me a tour. She told me I would be working with two other girls who had signed up last week.

But what I wanted to know was WHO in their right mind would sign up to shelve library books as an EXTRACURRICULAR ACTIVITY?!

At least I had a good excuse.

I did it while I was temporarily INSANE from MacKenzie's icy stare, which had frozen my brain cells, slowed my heartbeat and totally immobilised my body so I couldn't sign up for the avant-garde art competition.

I had the most horrible accident in French class today. While I was taking my French textbook out of my backpack my perfumed body spray, called Sassy Sasha, fell on the floor.

Unfortunately, the little white nozzle thingy popped off and it just kept spraying and spraying until the entire can was empty.

My teacher, Mr Somethin' or Other (I can't pronounce his name because it sounds like a sneeze), started yelling a lot of stuff in French that sounded to me an awful lot like swear words.

Then he evacuated all the students from the classroom, because everyone was coughing and choking and their eyes were watering really bad.

And while we were standing in the hallway, waiting for the smell to go away, he asked me very rudely in English (which I DO understand) if I was trying to KILL him.

Okay! First of all, I don't like French class that much anyway. And second of all, it was JUST an accident!

I mean, it's NOT like my perfume was REALLY going to kill him. At least, I don't *think* so.

But, then again, WHAT if it actually DID?! What if my French teacher collapsed in the teachers' lounge while eating a corn dog at lunch and died from extreme Sassy Sasha asphyxiation??!!

And what if, for three whole days, no one noticed the foul odour coming from his dead body, since the

←STINK FUMES

school lunches normally smell a lot like rotting flesh?!

The police would launch an investigation and I would be the main suspect.

Then the *CSI: Miami* crime-scene experts would conduct scientific tests on my French teacher's nose hairs and find traces of Sassy Sasha.

They would figure out that I was guilty of fumigating him with a lethal dose of my body spray.

And then, what if the CSI team SECRETLY planted ALL of the physical evidence on . . . MOI??!

(BTW, MOI is French for "ME"!)

I'd end up getting the ELECTRIC CHAIR during my freshman year, which would really SUCK!

And then afterwards, I'd be, like, TOTALLY peeved because I missed drivers' ed class *and* my senior prom!

You gotta believe me,
I'm totally innocent!

I have nothing to hide.
Search my bedroom!

OMG! A DEAD BODY! How did HE get in here?!

Now that I think about it, Mr Somethin' or
Other just LOVES MacKenzie, because she's really
good at French and she can pronounce his weird
sneeze-sounding name.

I bet if she had dropped HER Sassy Sasha body spray in his classroom and the nozzle thingy popped off, he would NOT have yelled at her or accused her of trying to kill him.

But that's because MacKenzie is

MISS PERFECT!!

I bet she's even going to WIN the avant-garde art competition!

And afterwards, just out of spite, she'll probably check out like 189 books from the school library and then return them all the next day.

Of course I'LL be the one STUCK having to put each and every one of them away, since I'm a STUPID library shelving assistant!

My pathetic life is SO UNFAIR it makes me want to

SCREAM! ☹!!

Today everyone in the cafeteria was super-excited because MacKenzie was handing out invitations to her big birthday bash. The way Lisa Wang and Sarah Grossman were crying and hugging each other, you would think they were gonna be on *My Super Sweet 16* or something. It was beyond DISGUSTING!

MacKenzie's PHONY friends crying PHONY tears and giving each other PHONY smiles and PHONY hugs!!

LISA → WANG

← SARAH GROSSMAN

They reminded me of the Olsen twins. For the life of me I never understood why those sisters were always hugging each other. They were the first set of non-Siamese twins who people actually thought were joined at the hip.

For the rest of the day everyone MacKenzie invited to her party sucked up to her like a human vacuum cleaner. Except for **Brandon Roberts**.

When she gave him an invitation she tried to flirt with him by twirling her hair around her finger and smiling really big. She even "accidentally" dropped her purse so he would pick it up for her, just like Tyra says to do when you're trying to get a guy to notice you.

But Brandon just glanced at MacKenzie's invitation, shoved it into his backpack and walked right past her.

And, boy, did she get upset when he blew her off like that.

Then, a bunch of jocks trampled all over her new $300 Vera Bradley bag before she could pick it up off the floor. Personally I kind of liked the dirty footprints better than that boring floral pattern.

Anyway, Brandon is SOOOO COOOOL!!!

From what I can tell he seems to be kind of the quiet rebel type.

He's a reporter and photographer for the school newspaper and has won a few awards for his photojournalism.

Once he actually sat at my lunch table, but I don't think he noticed me staring at him.

Probably because his shaggy, wavy hair is FOREVER falling into his eyes.

And today in biology, when he asked if he could take a picture for the school newspaper of ME dissecting my frog, I almost DIED!!

I was shaking so badly I could hardly hold the scalpel.

And now every tiny detail of his perfect face is permanently etched in my mind.

THE BIOLOGY OF MY HEARTBREAK
By Nikki Maxwell

I see you in my dreams
in your favorite white
button-down shirt,
sitting across from me
in the cafeteria.
I've never seen anyone
eat fries so beautifully.

I see you in biology class,
taking pictures for
the school newspaper, when
you whisper to the depths of my soul,
"Hold the frog at an angle."

For it is only you
who can make a photo
of a dissected frog
seem so vibrant.
So alive. Yet dead.

It hurts to feel this way,
to know that you'll never know me.
To want to run my fingers
through your dark, wavy hair,
as I realise that
the putrid smell of formaldehyde
and the dull gaze of a lifeless frog
will forever remind ME of US!

THURSDAY, SEPTEMBER 12

During my gym class even the Scared-of-Balls girls were gossiping about MacKenzie's party. Like one of them would ever get invited.

They're the really prissy girls who hang in small groups and scream hysterically whenever a ball comes near them.

It could be a basketball, football, baseball, soccer ball, tennis ball, volleyball, beach ball, Ping-Pong ball, mothball or even a meatball. They're NOT very picky.

SCARED-OF-BALLS GIRLS PLAY VOLLEYBALL

CHLOE and ZOEY   CHLOE and ZOEY freak out!

Red team WINS by 1 point! Your grade is A+. LOSERS, hit the showers! Your grade is C.

Gym → Teacher

Our team loses ☹!

YEP! You can always count on the Scared-of-Balls girls to screw things up and lose the game for you.

It really sucks to have girls like Chloe and Zoey on your team. Especially if you absolutely HATE taking showers after gym class (just the thought of showering at school makes me nauseous).

It will totally be THEIR fault if I catch some kind of incurable disease from the slimy mold and mildew growing in those NASTY showers.

WHY I *HATE* SHOWERING IN GYM CLASS!

Me → BEFORE showering . . . slightly sweaty but clean & fresh!

← Me AFTER showering . . . completely covered in stank, mildew, & slime!

I was really surprised when Chloe and Zoey came up to me after gym class and started talking. Of course, I pretended like I was NOT teed off at them for running away from the ball and making me have to take a shower.

Apparently our librarian, Mrs Peach told them I was assigned to work with them in the library and they were actually EXCITED about it.

Like WHAT is so exciting about shelving library books??!!

But I just played along and pretended to be as thrilled about it as they were.

I was like, "OMG! OMG! I can't believe we're going to be shelving books together. How COOL is that?!"

We ended up eating lunch together at table 9 and it was really nice NOT having to eat alone for once.

Chloe's full name is Chloe Christina Garcia and her family owns a software company. It was amazing because she has read like ALL of the latest novels.

She says she lives "vicariously" through the characters' joys and heartbreaks and learns a lot of stuff about life, love, boys and kissing, which she plans to use when she goes to high school next year.

She said she owns 983 books and has read most of them twice.

I was like, "WOW!"

Zoey's full name is Zoeysha Ebony Franklin and her mom is an attorney and her dad is a record company executive. She has met practically ALL of the biggest pop stars.

Zoey says she likes reading self-help and is currently seeking ways to "enhance" her relationship with the three "mother figures" in her life. She has a mom, a grandmother who helped raise her and a stepmother.

I was really sympathetic since I know from personal experience that having only ONE "mother figure" in your life can be traumatic and psychologically damaging.

Can you imagine having THREE?! OMG!

Then Zoey said, "How can you stand having a locker next to MacKenzie's? She is, like, so STUPID, she rubs lipstick on her forehead to make up her mind! And being really shallow can sometimes create multifaceted self-esteem issues."

I could NOT believe Zoey actually said that. I thought everyone at this school worshipped MacKenzie.

We laughed so hard that chewed-up carrot bits shot right out of my nose!

All three of us were like, EWWW! GROSS!

Then Chloe snickered, "Hey! Carrot-flavoured boogers! Let's give them to MacKenzie so she can sprinkle them over her tofu salad as a low-carb topping. In the Clique series, those girls are forever doing evil stuff like that to their frenemies."

We laughed so loud at Chloe's joke that the kids sitting at tables 6 and 8 started staring at us.

I even saw MacKenzie glance our way. But then she looked away really fast so we wouldn't make the huge mistake of believing she actually acknowledged our existence. I could tell she was wondering what was going on.

So, now I'm thinking about forgiving Chloe and Zoey for that whole shower FIASCO in gym class. I actually had a pretty good day today!

☺!!

I was pretty SICK and TIRED of hearing about MacKenzie and her STUPID little party! But since she is in my geometry class and I sit right behind her, I knew I was just going to have to suck it up and deal with it. I was trying my best to ignore her when she turned around, smiled at me and did the STRANGEST thing!

She handed ME a bright pink invitation tied with a big white satin bow!

I gasped and almost fell out of my chair.

My brain was like

OMG! OMG! OMG!

It was the most beautiful thing I had ever seen, other than maybe that new iPhone I want.

Who would have thought that I would get an invitation to THE party of the year?!

Then it dawned on me that this might be some kind of really cruel JOKE.

I looked around the room for a hidden camera, half expecting Ashton Kutcher (I can't believe he's married to a woman older than my mom) to jump out of the closet and yell . . .

You just got PUNKED!!

Then I realised that most of the other girls in my class were staring at me with envy and disbelief.

It was really weird, because suddenly I noticed I had tiny lint balls all over my favourite hoodie.

And it made me feel self-conscious, so I tried to pick a few of them off.

None of MacKenzie's friends would be caught dead in a not-from-the-mall hoodie with lint balls on it.

So I made a mental note . . .

BURN CURRENT WARDROBE!

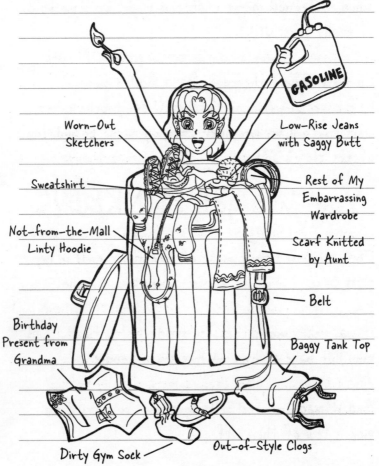

70

MacKenzie was still smiling at me like I was her new BFF or something.

"Hey, hon! I was just wondering if you would—?"

But I was SO excited, I jumped right in before she could even finish her sentence.

"MacKenzie, I would LOVE to!" I gushed. "Thanks for asking me . . . hon!"

Okay. So I actually called her "hon", even though I always thought that word sounded superphony.

And yes, I was totally GEEKED and as HAPPY as Vanessa Anne Hudgens when she found out she was NOT getting kicked off *High School Musical 3!*

But mostly I was in SHOCK. I could hardly believe I was actually going to MacKenzie's party! Soon I was going to have really cool friends and a social life. And maybe even highlights, a pierced belly button and a boyfriend.

I was starting to believe my *That's So Hot!* magazine was right. Maybe the key to happiness really was friends, fun, fashion and flirting!!

ME, floating on air amid sunshine, rainbows, twinkling stars and pink cotton-candy clouds, passionately clutching my invitation to MacKenzie's party over my heart!!

My hands were shaking as I untied the ribbon and tore open the envelope.

Suddenly, MacKenzie narrowed her eyes at me and scowled like I was something smeared on the bottom of her shoe.

"You IDIOT!" she hissed. "WHAT are you doing?!"

"Umm, opening m—my invitation?" I stammered.

I was already starting to have a really bad feeling about this whole party thing.

"Like I would invite you?!" She sneered, flipping her blonde tresses and batting her long lashes at me in disgust. "Aren't you the new girl who hangs around my locker all the time like some kind of creepy stalker?"

"Well, yes . . . I mean, NO! Actually, my locker is right next to yours," I muttered.

"Are you sure?" she said, looking me up and down like I was lying to her or something. I couldn't believe she was actually pretending like she didn't know me. I've only had a locker next to hers, like, FOREVER!

"I'm VERY sure!" I said.

Then MacKenzie took out her Krazy Kissalicious lip gloss and applied like three extra-thick layers. After gazing at herself in her little compact

73

mirror for two whole minutes (she is SO STUCK on herself!) she snapped it shut and glared at me.

"Before you so RUDELY interrupted me, I was simply asking if you would PASS my invitation to JESSICA! How was I supposed to know you were going to rip it open like some uncivilised GORILLA?" Mackenzie spat.

Then everyone in the class turned around and stared at me.

I could NOT believe my ears! How dare that girl

actually call me UNCIVILISED!!

"Oh. Okay. MY BAD!" I said, trying to sound coolly nonchalant about the whole thing while blinking back tears. "Um, who's Jessica?"

Suddenly I felt a sharp tap on my shoulder.

I turned around to face the girl sitting in the desk behind me.

She had long blonde hair and was wearing pink, glittery lip gloss, a pink sweater, a pink miniskirt and a headband trimmed with fake pink diamonds.

If I had spotted her in Toys "R" Us, I swear I would have probably mistaken her for a new fashion doll:

↑ "TOTALLY TICKED-OFF" JESSICA

75

"I'm Jessica," she announced, rolling her eyes at me. "I can't believe you opened MY invitation!"

I was desperately trying to tie the satin ribbon back on when she snatched the invitation from my hand so violently, I almost got a paper cut.

I felt like a TOTAL RETARD! And, to make matters worse, I heard a few of the kids around me snickering.

This was absolutely THE most EMBARRASSING moment of my PATHETIC little life!!

And I had no doubt that, in just a matter of minutes, everyone in the ENTIRE school was going to be text-messaging gossip about me.

I was relieved when our maths teacher, Mrs Sprague, finally started class.

She spent the entire hour at the board reviewing how to calculate the volume of a cylinder, sphere and cone for our upcoming test.

HOW TO CALCULATE VOLUME

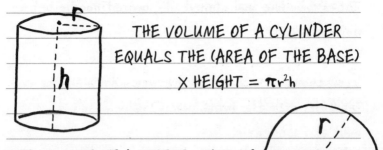

THE VOLUME OF A CYLINDER EQUALS THE (AREA OF THE BASE) × HEIGHT = $\pi r^2 h$

THE VOLUME OF A SPHERE = $4/3 \pi r^3$

THE VOLUME OF A CONE IS 1/3 THE (AREA OF BASE) × HEIGHT = $1/3 \pi r^2 h$

But I was too freaked out to concentrate on maths formulas and was totally NOT listening. I just sat there staring at the back of MacKenzie's head wishing I could disappear.

I guess I must have been really upset, because a tear rolled down my cheek and splattered my geometry notebook.

But I wiped it up with the sleeve of my not-from-the-mall, lint-ball-covered hoodie before anyone saw it.

Even though I was totally bummed about all the DRAMA over the invitation, I really wasn't that mad at MacKenzie.

I'M SUCH A LOSER!! If I was having a party, I WOULDN'T invite myself either!

SATURDAY, SEPTEMBER 14

I've had the most HORRIBLE week ever! WHY?

Because MacKenzie has been TRASHING my life:

1st She RUINED my chances in the avant-garde art competition.

2nd She DISSED me by NOT inviting me to her party.

3rd She RIDICULED me by calling me uncivilized.

4th She PUBLICLY HUMILIATED me by giving me an invitation and then UNINVITING me.

5th She tried to STEAL the one true love of my life, Brandon Roberts, by twirling her hair and flirting with him.

I planned to spend my ENTIRE weekend just sitting on my bed in my pajamas, STARING at the wall and SULKING.

Which, strangely enough,
always seems to make
me feel a lot better.

Me getting
my sulk on!

But my plans
were completely RUINED!

Around noon my mom came bouncing into my room
all cheerful and announced that for lunch we were
having a family cookout on the grill.

She said, "Honey, get dressed quick and come out
into the backyard and join the FUN!"

Well, obviously, I wasn't in the mood for "fun" and I
just wanted to be left alone.

And I didn't like hanging out in our backyard, because I have seen some fairly large spiders out there.

I have a thing about spiders — they creep me out.

Also, my physician has diagnosed me as being highly allergic to pests that suck human blood, such as spiders, mosquitoes, leeches and vampires.

My life motto is "Bloodsuckers CANNOT be trusted!"

Anyway, when I went outside my dad was all dressed up in his matching chef hat and apron that we got him for Father's Day.

It said "My Dad Is the World's Greatest Cook!" but most of the letters had faded off in the wash and it now says, "My Dad eat s ook!"

How we got that gift was actually kind of embarrassing. Mom drove me and Brianna to _Wal-Mart_ and gave us $30 to spend on a nice Father's Day present for Dad.

But after Brianna bought a "Tattoo-N-Tan" fashion doll for $9.99 and I bought the new Miley Cyrus CD for $14.00, we only had $6.01 left over to use for Dad, which wasn't a whole lot of money.

Lucky for us I spotted these hideous hot pink chef hats with matching aprons in a clearance bin for only $3.87.

We had a choice of "Kiss the Cook!", "When Mamma Ain't Happy, Ain't Nobody Happy!", "Detroit Pistons RULE!" or "My Dad Is the World's Greatest Cook!" in orange fluorescent lettering.

And since the gift was dirt cheap we still had, like, $2.14 left to buy a Father's Day card.

But I convinced Brianna that Dad would much rather have a handmade card from us that SHE could make for FREE using notebook paper, crayons and glitter.

She totally bought into it and I used the last few dollars to buy myself popcorn and an extra-large strawberry-mango smoothie. The snacks tasted good, considering the fact I was starving at the time and they came from a *Wal-Mart*.

Who woulda thunk Dad would have loved that tacky gift so much!

"This is the absolute BEST Father's Day gift I've ever received in my entire life!" he said and got all teary-eyed.

Which is NOT saying much, because every year Brianna and I outdid ourselves finding CRUDDY Father's Day gifts.

But we always managed to snag some really great swag for ourselves. Father's Day is now our favourite holiday after our birthdays and Christmas.

Anyway, my dad was grilling the meat while whistling old disco tunes.

Then, out of the blue, he suddenly developed a major complication. Not with his whistling, but his grilling.

I guess you could call it a bug problem.

So when he told me to run into the house and get the can of bug spray, I had a really BAD feeling about it.

I was like, "Dad, are you sure?"

And he was like, "I don't plan on sharing my twenty-dollar steaks with these pesky flies."

Well, THAT was a big mistake, because the bugs were NOT pesky flies.

BUG SPRAY

ZAP!

Roach & Ant Killer

NET WT 14 FL OZ

OUR FAMILY BARBECUE PICNIC
(A STORY IN PICTURES)

THE END

You'd think an experienced exterminator would recognise a fly when he saw one.

Unfortunately for Dad, he was dealing with a nest of very ANGRY HORNET WASPS!!

Well, our cookout ended up being a total disaster!

To make Dad feel better we all complimented him on how handsome he looked in his snazzy chef hat and apron, even though he was a little dirty from knocking over the neighbour lady's rubbish cans when he was running away from those wasps.

POOR DAD ☹!!

However, the good news is that I was able to go back up to my room and put in a few more hours of intense sulking. WOO HOO!

Today we had our maths test on calculating volume and I was really nervous. Mainly because I am not that good at maths.

The last time I got a decent grade in this subject was way back in first grade. And even then I almost got half the problems wrong.

It just so happened that I sat across from Andrea Snarkowski, the smartest girl in the entire first grade. We were taking a test on addition when I kind of "accidentally" noticed that Andrea's answer to one of the problems was different from mine. So, at the last minute, I decided to cross out my answer with an X and use the one she had come up with.

It was a good thing I did so, because I got an A on the test! My teacher was so pleased with my miraculous improvement — on a good day I usually did D+ work — she gave me a smiley face gold star. And only geniuses like Andrea Snarkowski earned smiley face gold stars.

Since I had morphed into a brilliant maths scholar, I also won the class Student of the Month Award and my picture appeared in our community newspaper.

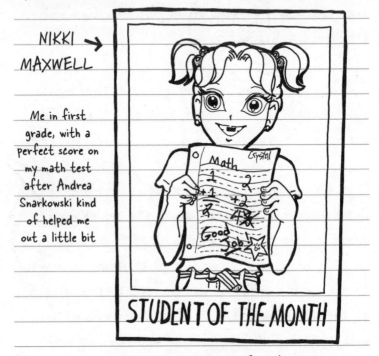

NIKKI → MAXWELL

Me in first grade, with a perfect score on my math test after Andrea Snarkowski kind of helped me out a little bit

STUDENT OF THE MONTH

My mom and dad were SO proud of me!

They made 127 copies of my newspaper article and mailed them out to every single one of my relatives all across the nation.

I can only imagine how happy and excited they

were for me when they opened their letters:

MY AUNT MABEL →

"Well, tutti my frutti! A picture of Dakota Fanning!"

MY UNCLE AUGUSTUS ↓

"It can't be! My long-lost nephew Vladimir, from Kazakhstan . . . ??!"

← MY GREAT-GRANDMA GERTRUDE

"Gracious, me! It's Bindi, the jungle girl!"

← MY THIRD COUSIN BILLY-BOB

"Ethel, call the cops! We just got another letter from that crazy stalker!!"

Okay, so maybe some of my relatives didn't recognise me right away.

But if they *had* I'm pretty sure they would have been really proud.

Anyway, my geometry test on calculating volume was really hard.

I know I should have studied more. But since I spent the entire weekend sulking, it kind of cut into my study time.

I pretty much just prayed like crazy through the whole test.

Sometimes even out loud:

"PLEASE, PLEASE, PLEASE HELP ME TO PASS
THIS TEST! I'M REALLY SORRY ABOUT SNOOZING
IN CHURCH LAST SUNDAY AND IT WON'T HAPPEN
AGAIN. ALSO, CAN YOU TELL ME IF THE
FORMULA FOR THE VOLUME OF A CYLINDER IS
$\pi r^2 h$ OR $\pi h r^2$? AND, WHEN YOU CALCULATE A
SPHERE, DO YOU MULTIPLY THE . . . ?"

I guess a few people sitting near me must have
overheard.

I was TOO happy when that test was *finally over!*

As I was putting my stuff into my backpack to go

to my next class, I couldn't help noticing MacKenzie eyeballing me all evil-like.

Then she walked up to Jessica and said, "Today is the last day to enter the avant-garde art competition and I have to take my entry form down to the office. I'll meet you at my locker. Okay, hon?"

Then Jessica stared at me and said really loud, "Mac, I just KNOW you're going to win first place. Your fashion illustrations are SO um . . . BOOTYLICIOUS!"

I could NOT believe Jessica said that, because "bootylicious" is like so yesterday!

But the thing that really freaked me out was when MacKenzie smirked at me and was all like, "Nikki, everyone in the entire school knows you're too CHICKEN to enter the art competition, because I'M a better artist than you are. So don't bother!"

Okay. Even though MacKenzie didn't actually SAY those words to me, she definitely looked like she was THINKING them.

And, either way, it was a humongous INSULT to my integrity.

Then she flipped her hair and sashayed out of the classroom. I just HATE it when MacKenzie sashays!

How DARE she talk about the art competition right to my face like that??!!

Especially when it was HER fault I DIDN'T enter to begin with.

93

This whole situation just TICKED me off!

Suddenly, I just totally lost it and screamed at the top of my lungs, "MacKenzie STARTED this WAR and now I'M going to FINISH it!!"

But I said it in my head, so no one else heard it but me.

Then I made a solemn promise to myself:

> I, NIKKI J. MAXWELL,
> being of sound mind and body,
> am officially entering the
> AVANT-GARDE ART
> COMPETITION!!

I was going to show MacKenzie once and for all that I had MAD art skillz. And MINE were WAY MADDER than HERS!

So I grabbed all my stuff and marched right down to the office to fill out an entry form.

Sure enough, MacKenzie was still in there applying

her fourteenth layer of lip gloss and bragging nonstop about her fashion illustrations.

". . . and everyone thinks my original designs are so HAWT and I'm going to be RICH and FAMOUS and move to HOLLYWOOD and blah–blah, blah–blah, blah–blah, blah!"

I was just casually chilling out behind a big plotted plant right outside the office door, minding my own business, when, *finally*, MacKenzie left.

But it was NOT like I was spying on her or anything.

I just didn't want to attract a lot of attention to myself or have MacKenzie think I was making a big deal out of the fact that I was entering the competition.

Although, to be honest, it WAS a big deal.

It was THE most important thing I had EVER attempted in my entire fourteen years of life here on planet Earth.

I rushed into the office and quickly filled out an entry form.

As I handed it to the assistant I felt a rush of panic, excitement and nausea, all mixed up together whirling around in my stomach like leftovers in a garbage disposal.

I walked out of the office and collapsed against the wall.

My heart was pounding so hard, I could hear it in my ears. I began to wonder if this whole thing was a big mistake.

Then, out of the blue, I got a really creepy feeling that someone was watching me even though the halls seemed empty.

Suddenly, a leaf on the plant I had hidden behind moved and I saw this EYE staring out at me! Then two eyes. Very icy-blue ones.

MacKenzie (YES, the MacKenzie) was peeping out at me from behind that big potted plant near the office door!

SHE WAS, LIKE, SO BUSTED!

Finally, MacKenzie climbed out of the plant and sashayed over to the drinking fountain like she was thirsty or something. But it was very obvious to me that she was just trying to use WATER TORTURE to FORCE me to change my mind about entering the art competition.

97

"OOPSY! MY BAD!"

MacKenzie tried to act all innocent and apologetic, like the whole squirting me with water thing was just an accident. But I looked into her beady little eyes and could tell she absolutely meant to do it.

I still could not get over the fact that I had actually caught her SPYING on me!

Which kind of made me ANGRY, because I don't follow her around SPYING on her and getting all up in her Kool-Aid (which, BTW, means "business").

Well, at least not that often.

Today was, like, *TOTALLY* an exception, mainly because we were both turning in entries for the art competition at the same time.

But to stoop so low as to SPY on me?!

THAT GIRL IS
ONE SICK
LITTLE PUPPY!

I can't believe I'm actually writing this while hiding in the janitor supply closet!! I know it's supergrungy in here and smells like an old, wet, mildewy mop, but I didn't know where else to go. I ABSOLUTELY

HATE! HATE! HATE! HATE! HATE! HATE! HATE! HATE! HATE! HATE! HATE! HATE!

THIS STUPID SCHOOL!!

Today at lunch I was carrying my tray and trying to get to table 9, where I was supposed to meet Chloe and Zoey. Things were going pretty good, because I had managed to sneak past the jock table without the football players making those embarrassing farting noises with their armpits.

But as I was walking past MacKenzie's table I really wasn't paying attention. She and Jessica must have STILL been pretty mad at me about the party invitation and the art competition, because this is what happened:

ME IN THE LUNCHROOM TRYING TO GET TO TABLE 9

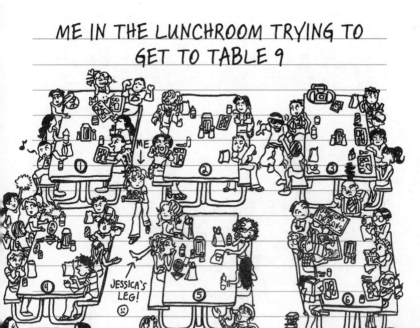

I tripped and suddenly everything started moving in slow motion. My lunch tray went flying up over my head and I heard a very familiar voice shrieking,

"Noooooooo!"

Then in HORROR, I realised it was MINE!

I fell flat on the floor and was so stunned I could barely breathe. My spaghetti and cherry jubilee dessert were smeared across my face and the front of my clothes. I looked like a life-size version of one of Brianna's messy finger paintings.

I just closed my eyes and lay there like a beached whale, with every inch of my body aching. Even my hair hurt. However, the worst part was that the *entire* cafeteria was laughing like crazy.

I was SO embarrassed, I wanted to DIE. I could barely see, because I had cherry jubilee in my eyes and it made everything look red and really blurry.

Finally, I gathered the strength to crawl to my knees.

But each time I tried to get up I slipped in the mixture of spaghetti and milk and fell back down again.

I have to admit, I probably looked hilarious sloshing around in my lunch like that.

And if it hadn't actually been happening to ME I definitely would have been laughing my butt off along with everyone else.

Then, MacKenzie folded her arms, glared at me and yelled,

"SO, NIKKI, ARE YOU HAVING A NICE TRIP?!"

Of course, that witty little comment made everyone laugh even harder.

It was the CRUELEST thing MacKenzie could have possibly said, especially since she was partially responsible for my "trip".

I was so humiliated, I started to cry.

The good news was the tears washed all the gunk out of my eyes and I could see again.

But the bad news was all I could see was this guy kneeling over me with a camera dangling in my face.

And only ONE person in the whole entire school owns a camera like that.

In a split second I knew *exactly* what was going to appear on the FRONT PAGE of the next issue of our school newspaper ☹!

And I was NOT going to be sending *that* article to any of my relatives.

WCD NEWS

25¢   FRIDAY, SEPTEMBER 13th

Lunchroom Disaster!

Eighth grader winds up messier than a sloppy joe

By Brandon Roberts

Nikki Maxwell,

It was very clear to me that some way, somehow, MacKenzie had completely charmed Brandon with her awesome beautyliciousness and lured him over to the DARK SIDE!

And then BRAINWASHED him!

How could my CRUSH – the secret LOVE of my life – do such a HORRIBLE and WICKED thing to me?!

I felt like I had been stabbed in the heart with my favourite lucky ink pen – the hot pink sparkly one

105

with the feathers, beads and sequins on the end —
and left to die. On the floor of the cafeteria.
With everyone watching. And laughing. By my beloved
BRANDON!!

Then the most bizarre thing happened!

Brandon kind of smiled at me, slid his camera out of
the way, grabbed my hand and pulled me up off the
floor.

"You . . . okay?"

I tried to say "Yes", but my voice just made a
gurgling sound like I was strangling or something. I
swallowed and took a deep breath.

"Sure. I'm okay. I had spaghetti for dinner
yesterday, but it wasn't nearly this slippery!"

I cringed. I couldn't believe I just said that. I am
such a RETARD!!

Then I watched, spellbound, as Brandon handed me

a napkin in what seemed like slow motion. I almost DIED, right there on the spot, when our fingers accidentally TOUCHED . . .

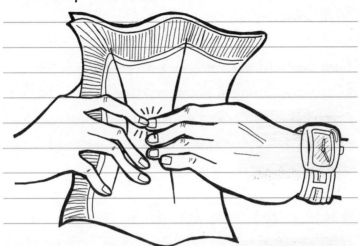

. . . ever so slightly, like a gentle but wild squirrel slurping sweet nectar from one of those dainty purpley flowers in my mother's garden that my dad accidentally sprayed with weed killer. Our eyes locked and for a split second it was as if we were gazing into the deep, misty cavern of each other's wounded souls. I will FOREVER remember the words he whispered into my trembling ear:

"Um . . . I think you have . . . something on your face?"

I blushed and my knees started feeling all wobbly.
"Probably my lunch . . ."

"Yeah, probably . . ."

Unfortunately, our very serious emo convo (which, BTW, means "emotional conversation") was rudely interrupted by Mr Snodgrass, our lunchroom monitor. But everyone calls him Mr Snot and a not-so-nice word.

He started cleaning up the mess on the floor and lecturing me about my responsibility as a young adult to keep my food on my tray at all times. Brandon rolled his eyes at Mr Snodgrass in a very chivalrous manner and then he kind of smiled at me again.

"I guess I'll see you in biology."

"Yeah . . . okay. And thanks. You know, for the napkin."

"Hey, no prob."

"Actually, we have napkins just like this at home.

My mom got them on sale. At Wal-Mart . . ."

"Oh, that's, um . . . cool. Well, later."

"Sure, see ya, in bio."

Then Brandon picked up his backpack and left the cafeteria.

I just clutched the napkin over my heart and sighed.

In spite of everything that had just happened, I suddenly felt VERY happy and butterflyish all over.

But that feeling lasted only about ten seconds, because that's how long it took me to notice MacKenzie.

MACKENZIE

She was SO angry, her whole face was all droopy and distorted.

She actually looked a little SCARY!

"I hope you're not STUPID enough to think HE'D like a LOSER like you?" she howled like a banshee.

But I guess I was still kind of disoriented, because I didn't have the slightest idea what she was talking about.

"Um . . . he, WHO?" I asked.

That's when Jessica blurted out, "You are such a KLUTZ. OMG! Look at her! I think she PEED her pants!"

And then MacKenzie was like, "OMG! You're right. She did PEE her pants!"

And both of them started laughing and pointing at me again.

I just rolled my eyes at them and said, "Yeah, right! I spilled MILK on my pants. Don't you morons know milk when you see it?"

Then I ran out of the cafeteria and went straight to the nearest girls' bathroom.

Inside there were about five girls at the mirror trying out one another's lip gloss flavours.

They completely froze and just stared at me in horror with their mouths wide open.

It was like they had *NEVER* seen anyone covered from head to foot in spaghetti and cherry jubilee before.

Some people are so RUDE!

I kind of staggered back into the hallway like a zombie. But instead of leaving a trail of slimy, rotted flesh I left a trail of spaghetti, sauce and cherry jubilee.

Then I noticed the door of the janitor's utility closet near the drinking fountain was cracked open a little bit. I peeked inside and, since no one was in there, I snuck in and closed the door.

I felt so HORRIBLE! That's when I burst into tears
and starting writing in my diary.

Pretty soon I heard some vaguely familiar voices
whispering and snickering outside the door.

I just knew MacKenzie and her peeps were trying to
track me down to harass me some more about peeing
my pants.

"Are you sure she's in there?"

"I think so. The spaghetti leads right up to this

door and stops. And look, cherry jubilee footprints! She *has* to be in there."

I was like, JUST GREAT!

At that moment I would have given anything to just DISAPPEAR into thin air.

Then they actually had the nerve to knock on my door. Well, not exactly *my* door, but the door to the janitor's closet.

I felt like the victim in one of those horror movies where the girl is home alone and hears a knock at the front door.

And when she goes to open the door everyone in the audience is yelling, "DON'T OPEN IT! DON'T OPEN IT!"

But she opens the door anyway because she doesn't *know* she's in a horror movie.

Who's that knocking?

Hey, maybe it's the pizza guy!

So . . . . you say you're giving out FREE haircuts?!

But I was NOT stupid!

I KNEW I was trapped in a horror flick so I

DIDN'T open the door to the janitor's closet. All of a sudden it got really quiet and I suspected it was a trick to make me think they had left.

But I had a feeling in my gut they were still out there.

"Nikki, are you okay?! We just heard what happened."

"Yeah, we wanted to make sure you were all right!"

That's when I finally recognised the voices.

It was CHLOE and ZOEY!!

Zoey said, "Girl, don't make me bust this door down, because you know I will do it!"

That kind of made me laugh, because Zoey has trouble opening her locker. And sometimes even her bottled water.

I was like, *Yeah, right!*

Then Chloe said, "If you're not going to come out and talk to us, we're coming IN!"

The next thing I knew Chloe and Zoey were poking their heads inside the janitor's closet and acting all goofy.

Chloe was snorting and giving me "jazz hands" and Zoey was sticking out her tongue and giving me the "stink eye".

They were like . . .

"WHAT'S UP, GIRLFRIEND!!"

For some reason seeing them made me start crying all over again. Soon, the three of us were just chilling out in the janitor's closet talking about all the drama with Jessica and MacKenzie.

But I left out the part about Brandon on purpose, because I was still kind of embarrassed about it. Plus, I was pretty sure he'd pick MacKenzie over me

any day. If I were a guy I sure would. I was so NOT
getting my hopes up about Brandon actually liking me.

Pretty soon the lunch period was almost over. Chloe
and Zoey helped scrub most of the food stains off

my clothes with paper towels and hand soap right at the big sink.

There were still some stains we couldn't get off though. I couldn't believe it when Zoey ran to her locker to get me her favourite lucky sweater to wear to cover them up.

And Chloe said that if I applied an extra amount of her Candy Apple Swirl ultrashiny lip gloss along with her midnight blue eyeliner, everyone (especially the guys) would notice my beautiful luscious lips and dreamy eyes instead of the pee stain . . . er . . . I mean, MILK stain on the front of my pants.

Which, lucky for me, was not that noticeable since it was starting to dry up.

In spite of how badly things went at lunch, I definitely feel a lot better now. I guess maybe I don't hate this school quite as much anymore. But I bet Brandon thinks I'm a

TOTAL KLUTZ!!

WEDNESDAY, SEPTEMBER 18

I think I'm suffering from Nomobilephoneaphobia.

I know it sounds like some really nasty disease where you're covered from head to toe with itchy, runny sores, or something hideous like that.

But it's actually the irrational fear of *NOT* having a mobile phone.

The worse thing about Nomobilephoneaphobia is that it sometimes causes hallucinations and makes you do insanely STUPID things.

I think I had an attack of this very debilitating disease on my way home from school today.

I thought for sure I saw a tiny, cute phone thingy that clips around your ear lying on the sidewalk near our mailbox.

I was like, SWEET!! A FREE phone thingy! It's ALL GOOD!

But when I took a closer look it was kind of a bright peachy colour.

I guessed that what I had found was actually a HEARING AID.

Of course, I was devastated when I finally figured this out because I was really pumped about having found a free phone thingy just lying there on the sidewalk.

I figured it probably belonged to Mrs Wallabanger, the little old lady who lives next door.

I suspected she was hard of hearing because for the past few days whenever I said, "Good morning", to her on my way to school, she would ask me to repeat what I said like seven times.

She has a scrawny lil' Yorkie named Creampuff and she walks him twice a day.

Creampuff looks like a fuzzy ball of lint on four legs, but he's as vicious as a Doberman.

Anyway, I spent five minutes trying to decide whether or not to knock on Mrs Wallabanger's door and ask if she had lost her hearing aid. But I figured if she HADN'T it would be a waste of my time and energy. And if she HAD it would be an EVEN BIGGER waste of my time and energy. I was right. This is what happened:

ME
(Talking very loud)

MRS WALLABANGER
(Not really hearing me)

GRRRRR!!
GRRRRR!!

CREAMPUFF
(Growling and trying to bite me)

WHAT I SAID	WHAT SHE SAID
Hi, Mrs Wallabanger. I just stopped by to ask if you lost your hearing aid?	What did you say, missy?
Your HEARING AID!! Is it lost?	Eh? Speak up, why don't cha?
Did you lose your HEARING AID?!	Eh? You say, I need to lose my HAIRY LEGS . . . ?!!
HEARING AID!! HEARING AID!!	Don't get fresh with me, you little whippersnapper!! My HAIRY LEGS are NONE of your BEESWAX. GET OFF MY PROPERTY!!

I was like, "Never mind!" My little chat with Mrs Wallabanger did NOT go well. So I figured I'd just hold on to her hearing aid for a while. Since she only comes out of her house to walk her dog, what's the WORST that could happen?!

"Hey, lady! Be careful! Don't step in that big pile of . . . !"

"Didn't you hear me, ma'am? I said, watch out for the WET CEMENT!!"

"Creampuff, dear, is that sound the mating call of the yellow-bellied swamp goose?!"

Okay, so maybe the WORST that could happen is Mrs Wallabanger gets run over by a truck!

But could you really say it was MY fault?!

Today, my social studies teacher, Mr Simmons, reminded the class that our project on how recycling can help stop global warming is due on Monday. I didn't have the slightest idea what I was going to do. I figured I'd just wait until my creative juices started flowing and come up with something the night before, like I always do.

Anyway, at lunchtime, I saw a group of CCP girls crowded around MacKenzie raving about her brand-new Prada mobile phone. And, get this! She had a phone thingy clipped on her ear that looked almost identical to the hearing aid I had found.

Even though I was starting to feel a little guilty about keeping Mrs Wallabanger's hearing aid, I suddenly got this fantastically brilliant idea for my social studies project. My project was going to:

1. encourage recycling to cut down on pollution

2. help stop global warming by reducing the number

of "hot air bags" yakking nonstop on mobile phones

3. boost my popularity at school by making everyone think I owned an expensive new phone thingy, just like MacKenzie's

I borrowed my dad's video camera and taped my project.

HOW TO MAKE A FAUX PHONE THINGY FROM AN OLD HEARING AID

(A Social Studies Project by NIKKI MAXWELL)

Hi, I'm Nikki, and I'm going to show you how to make a faux phone thingy from an old hearing aid. The word "faux" is pronounced "pho" as in "phony". It's a French word snobby people use that means "fake" or "knockoff".

STEP ONE:
GATHER YOUR SUPPLIES

For this project you will need:

● 1 hearing aid (recycled, found or "borrowed")
● 1 paper plate
● 1 can of spray paint (black or silver depending on the model you plan to make)

STEP TWO:
PAINT YOUR HEARING AID

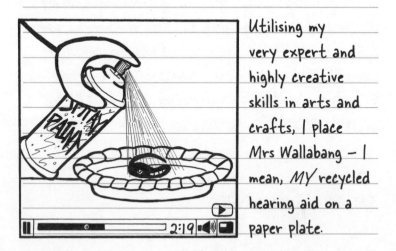

Utilising my very expert and highly creative skills in arts and crafts, I place Mrs Wallabang — I mean, MY recycled hearing aid on a paper plate.

Then I carefully spray paint it a shiny, metallic black.

Next, I allow the paint to dry for thirty minutes.

Recycling is a vital step in stopping global warming, as my very fine teacher, Mr Simmons, has taught our social studies class. [Waves to Mr Simmons.]

STEP THREE:
MAKE UP A SCRIPT FOR YOUR FAUX CALLS

Even though your phone thingy will look so real it'll fool your family and friends, you must always keep in mind that it is NOT real. This means you will have to make up faux (phony) things to say while you are wearing it, like:

1. "Dee-dee-dee! Dee-dee-dee!"
(This is your phone ringing. I recommend using a very high-pitched voice for authenticity. Or you can sing or hum your favorite song for a Top 40 ring tone.)

2. "*OMG!* I CAN'T believe she actually said that! I'm going to hang up and call (insert the name of your biggest school gossip) right now!"

3. "I'd really love to give you my mobile phone number, but I get SO many calls that my 'rents said I'm not allowed to give it out anymore or they'll take away my phone. But, if you like, I can put you on my waiting list to receive it . . ."

4. "Hello? Hello? Can you hear me now? You're breaking up! Hello?!"

5. "#@$%&!! Another dropped call! I HATE having (insert the name of a cruddy phone company) as a service provider!"

6. "Hello, I'd like to order a large pizza with extra (insert favorite pizza toppings) and hold the (insert least favorite pizza toppings). Thanks!"

7. "SHOOT! This stupid thing isn't working anymore! Either my battery is low or I need to buy some more minutes. Sorry!"

(The very convincing lie you tell when someone asks to borrow your cool phone to make a quick call. REMEMBER, IT'S *NOT REAL!*)

STEP FOUR:
CLIP YOUR FAUX PHONE THINGY ON YOUR EAR AND START TALKING.

5:32

Congratulations!

Your new faux phone thingy is now ready for public use!

IMPRESS your family and AMAZE your friends.

But most importantly, do YOUR part to help STOP global warming by recycling an old hearing aid into a faux phone thingy today!

THE END

Unfortunately, I had a little complication with step four. After dinner I decided to practise humming my ring tone so I could start receiving faux calls in school tomorrow. I had been wearing my phone for only about five minutes when I felt a mild irritation and burning sensation on my right ear and the area around it.

However, after ten minutes, it turned into a full-blown rash. A really itchy, irritating one.

It didn't take long for me to come to the conclusion that the rash was all my MOM'S fault!

Why she never bothered to tell me I was highly allergic to shiny, metallic black spray paint, I'll never know. I mean, she HAD to have known this information. Right? This is the same woman who gave birth to me!

Lucky for me, my dad still had some antihistamine cream left over from the time he got attacked by those wasps. So I slathered it all over my ear and the side of my face.

Since I had no further use for Mrs Wallabanger's hearing aid, I decided the moral and right thing to do was to return it to her.

ANONYMOUSLY!

I placed her hearing aid in a little box with a bow on it and attached a note. Then I put it on her front step, rang her doorbell and ran away. It's not like I was scared of her or anything. I just kind of wanted it to be a surprise.

Later that evening I saw Mrs Wallabanger walking her dog and, sure enough, she was wearing her hearing aid and a huge smile.

To:
Mrs.
Wallabanger ☺

If I EVER find another hearing aid on the sidewalk,
I'm definitely going to just leave it there. I only
hope:

1. I get a decent grade on my global warming project
and

2. This ugly rash goes away before school tomorrow

ICK! ☹!!

I was up and getting ready for school when I noticed I *STILL* had that rash from my faux phone! I almost choked on my minty-fresh, tartar control, extra-brightening, mouthwash-strength, cavity-fighting, gel toothpaste.

Now that my crush, Brandon, had *finally* noticed I was alive there was NO WAY I was going to school with a rash that made my ear look like it belonged to a severely sunburned Keebler Elf. You know, the ones who bake cookies inside a tree trunk infested with ants, termites, centipedes and beetles. I always wondered what those brown crunchy things were in their cookies. Ewwww!

Anyway, I knew my mom was NOT going to let me stay home from school unless I was spiking a temperature of at least 289 degrees. Which, BTW, is the same temp she uses to bake her Thanksgiving turkey.

MOM'S TEMPERATURE REQUIREMENTS FOR A THANKSGIVING TURKEY AND A SICK DAUGHTER

←289°→

My mom's life motto is, "Hey! Why let a little case of gangrene or leprosy get in the way of achieving a good education?!"

After trying every trick in the book I finally figured out how to convince my mom I was too ill to go to school. I had to PRETEND to throw up all over myself.

Now, how SICK is THAT?!

I came up with this idea last spring after Brianna had the stomach flu. Mom took time off from work and let my little sister stay home from school for an entire week.

On top of that she totally pampered Brianna by buying her all of her favourite Disney movies on DVD and a new computer game to keep her occupied while she was in bed.

I think all that vomiting must have really got to Mom. About three weeks later I stayed home from school with a bad case of strep throat and was

hoping to at least get a couple of new CDs out of it.
But all Mom bought me was a cruddy box of Popsicles!
And, to make matters worse, they were the really
gross low-calorie kind with no sugar. They tasted like
frozen pickle juice on a stick. I was like delish! ☹

Thanks a million, Mom!

But I have to
admit, Brianna
WAS a lot sicker
than I was. She
couldn't keep
anything down, not
even water!

I refused to
go anywhere
near her
unless I was
suited up in
full "puke
protection"
gear:

← Me ready for Brianna's
projectile vomiting due to
her stomach flu. Yuck!

Since I was pretty sure Mom was not going to consider my rash serious enough to let me stay home from school, I decided to run downstairs and make a quick batch of phony vomit, aka, "faux puke". Which I needed because of the rash caused by my faux phone. It was just another one of life's surprising little ironies.

Lucky for me, I was the first one out of bed, which meant I had the kitchen completely to myself for about fifteen minutes. Since things were going to get a little messy, I changed into my old heart pj's and rushed downstairs.

My secret recipe was easy to make and it looked and smelled like the real thing:

STAY-HOME-FROM-SCHOOL FAUX VOMIT

1 cup of cooked oatmeal

$1/2$ cup of sour cream (or buttermilk ranch dressing or anything that smells like rancid, sour milk)

2 chopped cheese sticks (for chunkiness)

1 uncooked egg (for authentic slimy texture)

1 can of split pea soup (for putrid green colour)

1/4 cup of raisins (to increase gross-osity)

Mix ingredients and simmer over low heat for 2 minutes.

Let mixture cool to warm vomit temperature. Use liberally as needed.
Makes 4 to 5 cups.

WARNING: This stuff is SO gross that it might really make you sick to your stomach and cause you to really throw up. In which case you will really need to stay home from school ☹!

I poured about 2 cups into a bowl, ran back upstairs to my room and dumped it down the front of my heart pj's. Then I yelled down the hall in a really whiney voice:

"MOM! Please come quick! I don't feel so good. My stomach is really queasy and I think I'm going to . . .

blecchuuarggh!"

Of course, it worked like a charm ☺!! Mom was totally convinced and said that not only did I have an upset stomach but also there was a mild rash on my ear.

She said that since I was not running a temperature, I'd probably feel better after a day of bed rest. I told her that suddenly I was feeling a lot better already (wink wink). Then she cleaned up my "mess", helped with my bubble bath and tucked me back into bed with a kiss.

I actually slept until the Tyra Banks show came on at noon. I just LOVE that girl!

However, when I went into the kitchen to grab a bite for lunch, I suddenly realised I had totally FORGOTTEN to pour the leftovers of my faux vomit down the garbage disposal.

So when I saw that my mom had left a note for me on the counter, right next to the now empty pot of puke, I just KNEW she was onto me and I was in really BIG trouble. I totally panicked and my stomach started feeling queasy, but this time FOR REAL! Her note said:

Dear Nikki:

Thank you for making breakfast for us even though you were not feeling well this morning. Your oatmeal was delicious and we all had seconds. You MUST cook this for us again soon. We are so very lucky to have such a KIND and CONSIDERATE daughter! Thanks again.

Love,
MOM ☺

P.S. Hope you're feeling better!

LOVELY ACCENTS©

I spent the entire afternoon just lounging around, watching television and raiding the fridge. I even ordered a pizza!

ME GETTING
MY GRUB ON
☺!

Plus, I had THREE things to be VERY happy about:

1. The Tyra Banks show ROCKED!

2. My rash completely cleared up.

3. My parents think I'm a fourteen-year-old
Rachael Ray.

I think Chloe and Zoey have totally lost their minds!

First of all, they practically freaked out when Mrs Peach announced she was taking six of her most hardworking and committed LSAs on a five-day field trip to the New York City Public Library to participate in National Library Week.

From what I understand it's like a big Mardi Gras celebration for people obsessed with libraries. Mrs Peach is already making plans, even though it's in April, which is still a whole seven months away.

But when Mrs Peach said there was going to be a "Meet-n-Greet" with a lot of really famous authors like Kate Brian, Scott Westerfeld, D. J. MacHale and some guy I've never heard of (Zoey said he was Dr Phil's son and her FAVE self-help guru for teens), Chloe and Zoey actually started jumping up and down and screaming their heads off.

I was like, "Girlfriends, take a CHILL PILL, PUH-LEEZE!"

MRS PEACH'S ANNOUNCEMENT . . .

I mean, I was excited, but not THAT excited. Now, if Mrs Peach had announced she was taking us to NYC to have a "Meet-n-Greet" with, like, the Jonas Brothers, Kanye West AND Justin Timberlake, I'd

have hyperventilated, fainted and rolled around on
the floor having seizures.

WHAT I *WISH* MRS PEACH HAD ANNOUNCED . . . !

Chloe and Zoey are really nice and sweet friends.
But I have to admit that sometimes they are . . .
like . . . SO WEIRD!!

The whole time we were shelving books they were talking nonstop about how we needed to do something really special to convince Mrs Peach to select the three of us for the trip to NYC.

"Well, why don't we just try to be the MOST hardworking and committed LSAs?" I suggested. "And we could start by maybe dusting off the books."

It was a no-brainer to me.

But Chloe and Zoey both looked at me like I was crazy.

"ALL of the other LSAs are going to be doing boring stuff like THAT to impress her!" Chloe groaned.

"Yeah! We need to come up with a secret plan that will blow Mrs Peach's mind!" Zoey said excitedly.

Okay, so dusting the library books was NOT exactly a mind-blowing idea. But it definitely would have solved my little sneezing problem.

We were putting out a batch of brand-new magazines when Chloe swiped a *That's So Hot!* and buried her nose in it. Suddenly, she gasped and then shrieked:

"OMG! This is *exactly* what we should do!"

"What? Get makeovers and become teen supermodels?" I asked sarcastically.

"NO! Of course not!" Chloe said, rolling her eyes at me.

"I know! I know! Make. Your. Face. Zit. Proof!"

Zoey said, reading one of the captions printed on the magazine cover.

"No way!" Chloe said. "Not that!" She was so excited, her eyes were practically bulging out of their sockets. Then she shoved the magazine in our faces and pointed.

". . . THIS!!"

Me and Zoey were like, "TATTOOS?! Are you NUTS?!"

"A tattoo promoting reading would be PERFECT! And it would show that we're serious and committed. Then Mrs Peach will choose us for the field trip for sure!" Chloe squealed.

"That's a WICKED idea!" Zoey said, staring in awe at the beautiful, tattooed model in the magazine.

"I bet we're going to look as cool as her once we get ours! *SWEET!*"

Okay. I could deal with going on a boring field trip for National Library Week. But there was just no way I was getting a tattoo to *CELEBRATE* going on a boring field trip for National Library Week. I mean, *WHAT* kind of tattoo would I even get?

I had to think fast. "Um . . . I agree this is *the* coolest idea, you guys. But I just found out a few days ago that I'm . . . superallergic to . . . spray painted hearing aids."

Chloe and Zoey looked really confused.

"Why would anyone spray paint a hearing aid? That's like SO bizarre!" Chloe said, shaking her head like I was really pathetic. Zoey agreed.

That's when I lost it and yelled at them both, "You know what I think is BIZARRE? Bizarre is getting a TATTOO for National Library Week!!" But I just said that inside my head, so no one else heard it but me.

"Well, spray paint and tattoo ink are *both* kind of . . . um, colourful, so I'm pretty sure I'm allergic," I said. "Which is really unfair because I was totally looking forward to getting a tattoo one day before I die."

"Well, if it's a medical problem, we understand. Right, Zoey? Hey! Why don't you help us pick out our tattoos?" Chloe was trying to make me feel better.

"Yeah, we should ask our parents to take us to get them this weekend!" Zoey said excitedly. "I can hardly wait to see the look on Mrs Peach's face when she sees our tattoos!"

But I already knew what her face was going to look like when she saw Chloe and Zoey . . .

POOR MRSS PEACH!! ☹

TUESDAY, SEPTEMBER 24

I was hoping Chloe and Zoey were over their wacky idea of getting tattoos for National Library Week. Thank goodness their parents said, "No way!" But when I saw them in gym class, they were still pretty upset.

Our gym teacher divided us up into groups of three for our ballet skills test and, at first, I was happy that me, Chloe and Zoey were together. Each group was supposed to pick classical music from the teacher's CD collection and then make up a short dance routine using the five ballet positions we had learned over the past weeks. Since I knew all of them I was sure I was going to get an A or, at lowest, maybe a B+ on the test.

ME DEMONSTRATING
MY AWESOME
BALLET TECHNIQUE

152

But, unfortunately, Chole and Zoey were too depressed to participate.

I was like, "Come on, guys, cheer up! We have to make up our ballet routine and practise it before we run out of time." But both of them just stared at me with big sad puppy-dog eyes.

"I can't believe our parents won't let us get tattoos! How unfair is that?" Chloe whined.

"And now Mrs Peach will NEVER pick us for the trip to NYC! It's like our hopes and dreams have shriveled up and DIED!" Zoey sniffed, wiping a tear.

They spent the next forty-five minutes venting and I, being the sensitive and caring friend that I am, sat quietly and listened.

Then the gym teacher came over and told us she was ready to start grading and we were going to be the second group to go. I just about had a heart attack because we hadn't selected any music or made up a routine.

I ran over really quick to grab a CD and the only one left was *Swan Lake*. And since I had seen MacKenzie looking at it a few minutes earlier, I was definitely a little suspicious. So the first thing I did was pop open the CD case and peek inside. I was surprised and relieved to see that a CD was still in there. Hey, I didn't trust that girl as far as I could throw her.

MacKenzie's group was first and I have to admit they were pretty good. But it wasn't due to their awesome talent. Combined, the three of them had, like, eighty-nine years of private lessons. They danced to "Dance of the Sugar Plum Fairy" and ended their routine like this:

What a bunch of SHOW-OFFS! I mean, what real classically trained ballerina would end her dance by doing splits and cheesing (which, BTW, means smiling) like she just got her braces off or something. I was like, "Hey, girlfriends! This AIN'T _Dancing with the Stars!_" But I just said it inside my head, so one no else heard it but me.

We were up next and I started getting butterflies in my stomach. Not because I was nervous. I just really hated humiliating myself in public. Chloe must have seen the look on my face because she whispered, "Don't panic! Just follow my lead. I took ballet lessons for three weeks back in second grade!" I said, "Thanks for sharing that, Chloe. Now I feel SO much better!" ☹

Then Zoey whispered, "What lies behind us and what lies before us are tiny matters compared to what lies within us. Ralph Waldo Emerson." Which, of course, had NOTHING WHATSOEVER to do with ANYTHING!

I had a really bad feeling about our routine and

we hadn't even started it yet. Mainly because I discovered our *Swan Lake* CD was actually NOT a *Swan Lake* CD. It said *Swan Lake* on the case, but the CD inside said something else. When I read the title, I was like:

It was *Thriller* by Michael Jackson!

Then my teacher snatched the CD out of my hand and popped it into her CD player and told us to take our places in front of the class.

I was about to explain that we had a slight complication with our music, but I got distracted when MacKenzie's group started squealing and hugging each other. They had got an A+ on their routine. But it was not like I was jealous or anything. I mean, how totally juvenile would *that* be?

Anyway, when our music came on Chloe must have completely forgotten we were supposed to be doing a ballet routine because she started doing some funky dance moves like she was one of those half-rotted zombies from the *Thriller* music video.

The next thing I knew Zoey was acting like a zombie too so I didn't have a choice but to follow along. Plus, I figured our teacher would probably knock a few points off our grade if Chloe and Zoey were staggering around like the undead and I was doing ballet pliés in first and third position.

Okay. I really, really like Chloe and Zoey. But while I was up there dancing with them, I couldn't help thinking, "What am I? Flypaper for FREAKS?!"

I had to keep reminding myself that this whole thing was MacKenzie's fault, not THEIRS.

ME, CHLOE, AND ZOEY IN
BALLET OF THE ZOMBIES!

Actually, I was surprised that Chloe and Zoey were such good dancers. It looked like our gym teacher was pretty impressed too, because when we finished, she just stared at us with her mouth open and started tapping her ink pen on her clipboard really fast. Then she asked us to see her after class. We were really nervous when we went up to talk to her because we didn't know what to expect. Chloe and Zoey thought maybe she was going to ask us to join the school's dance squad, since she was the assistant coach. I was keeping my fingers crossed on that one because dance squad meant automatic membership in the CCP clique.

Our teacher smiled and said, "Girls, if we were doing the section on contemporary dance, you would have definitely got an A+!"

After hearing that I was pretty sure she was going to give us a good grade on our routine even though we had made it up on the spot and with the wrong music.

Then our teacher stopped smiling.

"The three of you were supposed to be doing classical ballet, but you weren't even close. The highest grade I can give you is a D. I'm really sorry."

We were like, OH. NO. SHE. DIDN'T!!
Me, Chloe and Zoey were CRUSHED! (LITERALLY)

Then I screamed at my teacher, "Are you NUTS?! How in the world can you give us a D? Do you even realise how tricky those dance steps were? It was definitely A LOT harder than it looked! Let me see YOU try to moonwalk like a zombie, sister!"

But I just said all of that in my head, so no one heard it but me.

And get this! *Then* our teacher had the nerve to tell us to "hit the showers"! Like, what did showering have to do with classical ballet?! ABSOLUTELY NOTHING!!

I was a little peeved at Chloe and Zoey, because if they had NOT been wasting time whining about tattoos and National Library Week we could have made up a decent ballet routine to the correct music and maybe earned at least a C. But *NOOOOOO!*

Then, at lunch, things went from bad to worse. Chloe and Zoey had a

TOTAL MELTDOWN!

They actually came up with this elaborate scheme to run away from home and live in the secret underground tunnels beneath the New York City Public Library!

But the crazy part was that they planned to leave this Friday and then just "hang out" for seven whole months until National Library Week rolled around in April.

They figured that, by arriving early, they'd get in FREE and be FIRST in line for the author "Meet-n-Greet".

Chloe said residing at the library was going to be an "exhilarating experience", because they could read all the books they wanted, twenty-four hours a day, without having to check them out or reshelve them.

And Zoey said they were going to live off Diet Pepsi and nachos which they planned to SWIPE from the library snack bar each night!

I CANNOT believe Chloe and Zoey are actually going to do something so crazy, dangerous and illegal.

CHLOE AND ZOEY USING THEIR NATURAL INSTINCTS TO SCAVENGE FOR FOOD

And I plan to do everything within my power to STOP them!

WHY?!

Because Chloe and Zoey are my BEST friends at this school!

And my ONLY friends at this school! But that's beside the point.

Unfortunately, I only have TWO options:

1. Rat them out to their 'rents and risk losing their friendship forever

OR

2. Figure out a way to get girlfriends some tattoos for National Library Week PDQ (which, BTW, means "pretty darn quick")!!

I hardly got any sleep last night! I kept having horrible nightmares about Chloe and Zoey living in the secret underground tunnels beneath the NYC public library.

In one of my dreams they were having a dinner party with some of their neighbours.

And in the scariest one I got married to Brandon Roberts and Chloe and Zoey were bridesmaids. But they brought a few uninvited guests to my wedding ☹!

OUR WEDDING

I actually woke up SCREAMING my head off until I realised it was all just a very bad dream!

THURSDAY, SEPTEMBER 26

This morning at breakfast my little sister, Brianna, got on my last nerve.

I was just sitting there eating my Cinnamon Life, reading the back of the cereal box and trying to figure out what I was going to do about the Chloe and Zoey situation.

They were planning to leave in less than twenty-four hours.

Brianna was eating Fruity Pebbles and drawing a face on her hand with an ink pen. She said she was naming the face "Miss Penelope" because she was "borned from a pen".

BRIANNA'S HAND

Even though I was trying to concentrate on my personal problems, Miss Penelope asked me to watch her perform "Itsy-Bitsy Spider", the Rihanna remix version.

Apparently, the itsy-bitsy spider went up the water spout, but got washed out by the rain because he had no umbrella, ella ella, eh, eh, eh!

The whole thing annoyed me to no end, because I wasn't that into puppet shows.

Anyway, I warned both Brianna and Miss Penelope to quit bothering me, mainly because I was in a really

HORRIBLE MOOD.

And it was not helping matters that Miss Penelope's awful singing sounded like a humpback whale in labour.

She must have been highly insulted by my unbiased critique of her singing abilities, because she hauled off and punched me on my arm.

So I grabbed Miss Penelope and tried to drown her in my cereal bowl.

I was like,

"Got milk?!"

Brianna started screaming, "Stop it! Miss Penelope can't swim! Let her go! You're smushing her face!"

But I wouldn't let go. That is, until my mom walked into the kitchen.

"Why on Earth are you shoving your sister's hand in your cereal?! LET GO OF HER THIS INSTANT!!"

So I released Miss Penelope, only because I didn't have a choice.

Brianna stuck her tongue out at me. "Miss Penelope says she's not inviting you to her birthday party! Na, na, na, na, na!!"

Then I stuck my tongue out at *her* and said, "I've *already* not been invited to a birthday party. SO THERE!" I could thank MacKenzie for that one.

Anyway, I think I taught Miss Penelope a good lesson. I bet she won't be interrupting my breakfast again anytime soon (EVIL GRIN).

Since my cereal had been contaminated by Miss Penelope's germs, I dumped it into the sink and ran upstairs to my bedroom.

I sat on my bed and stared at my wall as a million thoughts bounced around in my head.

I had to admit the Chloe and Zoey situation seemed hopeless and there was nothing I could do to fix it ☹.

To make matters worse Miss Penelope was still in

the kitchen singing so off-key, I thought my ears were going to bleed. I felt like taking my favourite pen – a water-based, nontoxic, dark-purple, gel ink pen by HotWriter, Inc. – and drawing a big fat zipper across her mouth to shut her up. But I was pretty sure my mom would have just YELLED at me again.

I mainly just use it to write in my diary and to bring me good luck. But lately the good luck part hasn't been working so well.

MY LUCKY PEN

I was twirling my pen in my fingers when, suddenly, the CRAZIEST idea popped into my head! I was like, OMG! This might work! I quickly scribbled out two notes and then rushed off to school fifteen minutes early to tape them on Chloe's and Zoey's lockers.

Meet me in the janitor's closet before class starts. It's really important!!

Nikki ☺

I waited in the janitor's closet for five long minutes and was starting to worry they were not going to show up. But finally they did.

"I hope you didn't ask us to come here to try and change our minds about running away," Chloe said, real seriouslike.

"Yeah! This is something we just gotta do," Zoey said, staring at the floor.

It got so sad and quiet, I thought I was going
to cry.

"Um . . . I asked you both to come here to
tell you about a special present I wanted to give
you on Monday. But since you're leaving
tomorrow . . ."

Of course, this made Chloe and Zoey really curious,
and they started begging me to tell them what
it was.

"Well, you may not know this, but I'm a pretty
decent artist. Not that I'm bragging or anything.
And since you guys are my BFFs, I've decided to
personally give you each a tattoo! Temporary ones. In
honour of National Library Week!"

At first Chloe and Zoey just stared at me like
they couldn't believe it.

Then they started screaming and jumping up and
down and hugging me.

ME, CHLOE AND ZOEY DOING A GROUP HUG!

"Just decide what kind you want," I said, "and I'll design it over the weekend and draw it during lunch on Monday. But you both have to make me one promise . . ."

"Anything!!" Zoey gushed. "Let me guess! We have to ditch our plans to run away and live at the NYC library?"

"Okay, then it's officially CANCELED!" Chloe announced and did jazz hands, like the show was over.

"Actually, that's not what I meant," I said, hiding my smile and trying to look all scary-serious. "I want you both to promise me you won't bring RATS to my wedding!"

"HUH?!" They both looked at me like I was crazy.

"Never mind!" I giggled. "It's a long story."

Before biology class started, I noticed Brandon was kind of staring at me, but I wasn't sure if it was my imagination or not. Lately, it seemed like whenever I looked at *HIM*, he was looking at *ME*.

But then we both would look away and pretend like we WEREN'T really looking at each other.

Well, today he actually smiled at me and said, "So, which cell cycle would you rather study? Mitosis or meiosis?"

I smiled back and kind of shrugged my shoulders because actually I HATED both of them EQUALLY. And I was afraid that anything I said would probably make me look like a BIGGER idiot than he already thought I was.

But the main reason I couldn't talk to Brandon was because I was suffering from a very severe and debilitating case of RCS, or Roller-Coaster Syndrome. Studies show that it mainly attacks girls between the ages of eight and sixteen.

The symptoms are difficult to describe, but whenever Brandon talks to me my stomach feels like I'm dropping three hundred metres at eighty miles per hour. Simply calling it "butterflies" is a common and dangerous misdiagnosis.

Suddenly, and without warning, I feel compelled to throw my hands up in the air (like I just don't care) and scream . . .

"WHEEEEEE!"

ME RIDING THE
LOVE ROLLER
COASTER!!
I so
LOVE to HATE
this feeling
☺!!

Then my day got even BETTER! While I was working in the library Brandon came in to return a book called *Photography and You*. I was just sitting there doodling a few tattoo designs for Chloe and Zoey, when he leaned across the counter and peeked at my notebook.

"Now *that* is good! I didn't know you were an artist!"

I looked around to see who he was talking to. Then, I totally freaked out when I realised he was actually talking to ME! I could hardly BREATHE.

"Thanks, but it's no big deal. I've been going to art camp, like, forever. And last summer, I got practically a million mosquito bites and wow did they ever itch!!" I babbled like an idiot.

"Well, one thing is for sure, you definitely got skillz!"

Brandon's hair was hanging in his eyes again as he smiled and kind of leaned in even closer to look at my sketches. I thought I was going to DIE! He smelled like Snuggle fabric softener, Axe body spray and . . . red licorice?!

I couldn't stop blushing and there was no way I could draw with him watching me like that. I started feeling that roller-coaster thing all over again . . . WHEEEEE!

Suddenly Brandon's eyes seemed to twinkle with excitement.

"Hey! Are you entering the avant-garde art competition? I'll be covering it for the newspaper."

"Yeah, I'm thinking about it. But everyone is saying MacKenzie's fashion illustrations are going to win this year. So I dunno . . ."

"MacKenzie?! Are you kidding? You have more talent in your smallest burp than she has in her entire body. I'm serious! You know that, right?"

I could NOT believe Brandon actually said that! It

was so rude. So wickedly funny. So . . . TRUE!

We both laughed really hard. I didn't know he had such a wacky sense of humour.

Soon, Chloe and Zoey came staggering up to the front desk, each loaded down with a stack of books that needed to be put away.

When they saw us their mouths dropped open.

They looked at me, then at Brandon, then at me again. Then at Brandon. Then back at me. Then Brandon. Then me. Then Brandon again.

This went on, like, FOREVER!

They were gawking at us like we were a new animal exhibit at the zoo or something.

It was SO embarrassing!

Brandon's smile went slightly crooked, but otherwise he acted coolly nonchalant about the whole thing.

"HEY, GET A LOAD OF THOSE TWO!
IT MUST BE MATING SEASON OR SOMETHING . . ."

"Hey, Chloe! Hey, Zoey!" he said.

But they were so shocked, they didn't even
answer him.

"Well, I better get back to class. See you later,
Nikki." Then he strolled out the door and
disappeared into the hall.

Chloe and Zoey made a big deal over Brandon talking to me like that and started nagging me to admit he was my secret crush.

After I made them both pinkie swear not to tell anyone, I told them about how Brandon had helped me up after Jessica tripped me in the cafeteria a couple of weeks ago.

Then I grabbed my backpack and unzipped the cute little pocket in the front and showed them The Napkin.

At first they just stared at it in awe. But soon they were teasing me and giggling like two kindergarteners. "Brandon and Nikki sittin' in a tree, K-I-S-S-I-N-G!"

I told them to shut up before someone overheard them and it got out all over the school.

Chloe insisted that I keep The Napkin for the rest of my life, because there was a chance that Brandon and I could accidentally meet up on some exotic, romantic island twenty years from now. She said it could happen just like it did in those chick flicks at the movie theatre.

MY BEST FRIEND'S NAPKIN
(SLEEPLESS IN SAN DIEGO)
Directed by Chloe Christina Garcia

BRANDON:
I couldn't help but notice you from across the room and be hopelessly drawn to your brains and beauty! It almost seems that we've met before. Perhaps in another place . . . another time . . . another life . . . !

ME:
Alas! Allergy season is upon us. Please! Take this most cherished napkin from my very heart-wrenching, mysterious past.
And do with it . . . what you must!!

ME:

What a powerful sneeze you have! It is aptly captured in this delicate napkin of forgotten love . . . now merely a disposable tissue drenched in lost and shattered dreams!

BRANDON:

Hark! Do mine eyes deceive me?! I'd recognize OUR napkin in even the darkest of murky depths! My joy and passion overwhelm me!

BRANDON:

Is it really you? My beloved, Nikki! Finally, I've found my TRUE LOVE! Will you MARRY ME?!

THE END

I told Chloe her story was really sweet and romantic. But if the napkin was really dripping with snot and Brandon proposed on the spot like that, MY story would probably have a different ending.

ME:
Gee, Brandon, I think we need
to take things a bit slower.
First, let's get rid of the
snotty napkin . . . ICK!!
Second, how about pizza and
a movie . . . ?

THE END

Zoey said she didn't blame me for rewriting Chloe's happy ending, because snot and airborne bacterial particles were the most common way of transmitting germs to others.

But Chloe complained we both *TOTALLY* missed her point. The Napkin, germy or not, should be cherished because it was a token of Brandon's love. And after reading *Twilight* she had learned that forbidden love, obsession and sacrifice could be very messy things. Just like snot.

I had to admit that Chloe had a really good point.

Then Zoey said I should always remember that guys are from Mars and girls are from Venus, because they think and communicate very differently, according to a book she was reading on dating. I was really surprised to hear this, because I thought for sure that Earth was the only planet with human life on it.

I'm really glad Chloe and Zoey know so much

about guys, dating, love and stuff like that.

Because I don't have a CLUE.

DUH!!

This is going to be my LONGEST diary entry
EVER! I have the most horrible headache and it's
all Brianna's fault. Why, why, why couldn't I have
been born an ONLY child?!

Okay. This is what happened: my mom and Brianna
were supposed to see a matinee movie today. But
Mom needed to go to the mall to buy a present
for a baby shower she was attending later this
evening.

So she offered me $10 to take Brianna to the
movie in her place. Since I was broke, I agreed to
do it. I figured that, at the worst, I could sleep
through the movie and earn $10 for a ninety-
minute nap.

The movie was called *Princess Sugar Plum Saves
Baby Unicorn Island! Part 3*. There must have been
four hundred squealing little girls there and half
of them were dressed up like princesses and
unicorns.

I should have charged my mom $50 for taking Brianna, because the whole event was so sugary sweet, it actually made me nauseous.

But Brianna thought the movie was superscary because there was a fairy in it. And she has this irrational fear that the tooth fairy is going to pull out all her teeth to make dentures for old people. I guess you could say she suffers from "fairy phobia".

Anyway, Brianna practically drove me CRAZY, because every time the fairy appeared on the screen, she got really scared, grabbed my arm and bumped my popcorn.

I must have dumped three whole boxes on the nice lady sitting next to me.

But when that nice lady looked like she was going to slug me I decided it would be safer to eat Raisinets instead.

I was TOO happy when that stupid movie was finally over.

Brianna and I were waiting near the main entrance for Mom to pick us up. However, when I saw Dad pull up in his Maxwell's Bug Extermination van I got a really bad feeling. Although, that creepy-looking roach bolted to the top of his van gave *most* people a really bad feeling.

BTW, the roach's name is Max (courtesy of Brianna, "because if I had a puppy, I'd name him Max.").

I was like, OH CRUD! If anyone from my school saw me getting into Dad's van my life would be over. I scanned the crowd for middle school kids and luckily it was still mostly three- to six-year-olds. "Hi, girls, hop in! Your mom's still shopping. I just got an emergency call so you get to ride along to keep me company," my dad said, winking.

I was like, "Um . . . thanks, Dad, but I have an awful lot of homework to do. So could you just drop me home first! PLEASE!" I was trying really hard to remain calm.

My dad glanced at his watch and frowned. "Sorry, but I don't have time to swing by the house. This customer is hysterical and has agreed to pay my emergency rates. She's hosting some kind of big shindig later today and says her house is crawling with bugs inside and out. Hundreds of 'em just showed up out of the blue this morning."

"ICK!!" Brianna said, scrunching up her nose.

"Sounds like a box elder infestation to me." Dad continued, "Hopefully, she's not throwing that baby shower your mom is supposed to be attending later today."

191

I grumpily climbed into the front seat of the van and tried to slouch down really low so no one could see me.

Whenever we stopped at a red light a bunch of people would point, stare and laugh. Not at me; at our roach.

For some reason Brianna thought all the gawkers were just being friendly. So she started smiling, waving and throwing kisses out the window like she had just been crowned Miss America or something.

And Dad was pretty used to all the rude stares. He just ignored them and hummed along to his *Saturday Night Fever* CD.

Thank goodness I noticed an empty grocery bag sticking out from under the seat.

Even though it said: WARNING: TO AVOID SERIOUS INJURY OR DEATH PLEASE KEEP PLASTIC AWAY FROM VERY YOUNG CHILDREN I poked two eye holes in it and pulled it down over my head.

First of all I *WASN'T* a very young child.

And second of all I'd rather suffer a slow and painful death by asphyxiation than be spotted riding around in the "roachmobile"!

I have to admit, we probably looked like a

FREAK SHOW ON WHEELS.

It was SO embarrassing!

I wondered how serious my injuries would be if I jumped from a moving vehicle travelling forty-five miles per hour. Assuming I survived I could at least walk home and end the humiliating ride in Dad's van.

About ten minutes later we drove up a long driveway that led to a huge house. Wow! Nice house, I thought. Too bad it has bugs!

Brianna stared at the house in awe. "Daddy, can I go inside with you? Pretty please!"

"Sorry, pumpkin, but you'll have to wait out here in the van with your sister and make sure no one steals Max, okay?"

Like, WHO in their right mind would want MAX?!

Two shiny black bugs about a half inch long landed on the window of our van.

"Yep! Box elders all right," Dad said, eyeing them carefully. "Basically just a harmless eyesore. To spray the entire premises will probably take about twenty minutes. But I'll try to get it done as fast as I can. If you girls need anything I'll be right inside."

Dad unloaded his equipment and lugged it up the front steps. Before he could ring the doorbell a frantic-looking middle-aged lady in designer clothing opened the door and ushered him in.

Brianna started to pout. "I wanna go in there with DAD!"

"NO! You're supposed to stay here. And watch Max! Remember?" I said sternly.

Brianna wrinkled her nose at me.

"YOU watch Max! I gotta go to the bathroom!"

"Brianna, Dad will be back real soon. Can't you just hold it a little longer?"

"NO! I gotta go NOOOWW!"

I was like, Just great! All of this drama for a measly $10.

"Okay, fine," I said, finally giving in. "When we go

inside don't touch anything. Just use the bathroom and come right out, got that?"

"I wanna say hi to Dad too!"

"No! You're gonna use the bathroom and then we're coming back to the van to wait for . . ."

Before I could finish my sentence Brianna slid open the van door and dashed to the front steps.

By the time I caught up with her she was already leaning on the doorbell. "Ding-dong! Ding-dong! Ding-dong!"

The flustered-looking lady answered the door again and looked surprised to see Brianna and me.

"Um . . . I really apologise for disturbing you," I stammered. "But we were out in the van waiting for our dad and—"

"Hey, lady! I gotta go PEEEEEEE!" Brianna interrupted.

Then she started squirming and making ugly faces
for maximum dramatic effect.

The lady looked at Brianna, then at me and then
back at Brianna. She stretched her thin red lips
into a strained smile.

"Oh! So your dad is our . . . exterminator. Sure,

honey, the bathroom is right this way. Follow me."

The inside of the house looked like something out of one of my mom's fancy home and garden magazines. We were headed down a hallway off the foyer when the lady stopped in her tracks.

"Oh, wait! There's bug spray in all the bathrooms on the main floor. You're going to have to use one upstairs. All of the bedrooms have an attached bathroom. I'd escort you myself, but my caterer is supposed to call me any minute now for a final head count."

The telephone rang and the lady gasped and rushed off, leaving us standing there. Brianna smiled and darted up the huge staircase ahead of me.

As she entered the first bedroom on the right she squealed with glee, "Ooh! Pretty!"

It was decorated in shades of pink and had plush carpeting soft enough to sleep on. The laptop and big-screen TV were to die for. My entire bedroom

198

could fit into the walk-in closet. But, personally, it was a little too sugar-n-spice for my taste. Not that I was jealous or anything. Like, how juvenile would THAT be?!

ME AND BRIANNA IN
TOTAL AWE OF THE FABULOUS BEDROOM!!
(WHICH, BTW, TOOK ME, LIKE, FOREVER TO DRAW!!)

"Hey! Can I jump up and down on this princessy bed?!" Brianna asked.

"NO!" I snapped. "Get down!"

It took all my willpower not to snoop. I wondered what school the girl attended and if we could ever be friends. I bet she had a perfect life. Unlike me.

Brianna skipped into the adjoining bathroom and locked the door behind her. "Wow, I'm gonna get a bathroom like this for my birthday!"

Soon, I heard the toilet flush. But after three minutes she still had not come out.

"Brianna, hurry up!!" I shouted through the door.

"Wait, I'm still washing my hands really good with this strawberry soap and then I'm going to put on some yummy-smelling cupcake body spray."

"Come on. We have to go back to the van now."

"Wait!! I'm almost done!"

Suddenly I heard a sickeningly familiar voice.

"But, Mommm! I CAN'T have my party with these horrible BUGS crawling all over! We should have had it at the country club like I wanted. This is totally YOUR fault!"

I almost wet my pants! It was MACKENZIE ☹!

I was like, OMG! OMG! OMG! Today was the party I had not been invited to.

It was like a demented nightmare. I was trapped in MacKenzie's bedroom, my sister was locked in MacKenzie's bathroom and my dad was exterminating MacKenzie's house. And if *all* that wasn't awful enough, our van, with a humongous roach on top of it, was parked in MacKenzie's driveway with MY last name plastered across the side of it (the van, not the roach).

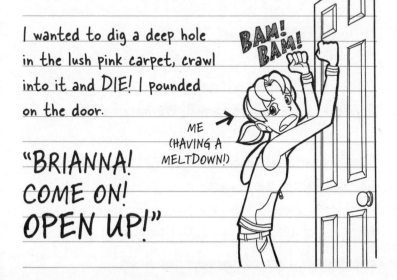

BAM!
BAM!

I wanted to dig a deep hole in the lush pink carpet, crawl into it and DIE! I pounded on the door.

ME → (HAVING A MELTDOWN!)

"BRIANNA!
COME ON!
OPEN UP!"

"I'm busy. Go away!"

"You've been in there long enough. Now open the door!"

"Say 'pretty please.'"

"Pretty please."

"Now say 'pretty please with sugar on top.'"

"Okay. Open the door, pretty please with sugar on top . . ."

"NO!! I'm NOT done yet!"

"Mommm! This party is going to be a DISASTER! My reputation will be ruined! We have to cancel it."

I could hear MacKenzie's shrieks getting louder. She was coming up the stairs!

"Brianna. Open the door quick! PLEASE! It's an emergency!" I hissed through the door.

202

"Wait! I'm putting on the yummy-smelling cupcake body spray now. Um . . . what's the emergency?"

Now MacKenzie was in the hallway.

"Mom, I'm calling Jessica. She'll never believe this is happening to me . . ."

I had exactly three seconds to convince Brianna to open the bathroom door.

"Brianna! It's the TOOTH FAIRY! She's coming and we have to get out of here!! NOW!!"

The lock on the door clicked and Brianna whipped open the door.

She looked even more afraid than she had been at the *Princess Sugar Plum* movie.

"D-did you say T-T-TOOTH FAIRY?!"

"Yes! Come on, let's HIDE! Quick!"

Brianna was panicking and starting to whine.

"Where is she? I'm scared! I want Daaaaaddy!"

"Let's hide behind the shower curtain. If we're really quiet, she'll never find us."

Brianna shut up instantly, but her eyes were as big as saucers.

I actually felt a little sorry for her.

We dove into the bathtub and huddled behind the shower curtain.

I could hear MacKenzie stomping around her bedroom and screaming into her mobile phone.

"Jess, there's no way I can have this party now! Our house is crawling with bugs! What? . . . How am I supposed to know what they are? They're these big, black, er . . . roaches or something. Some guy is here spraying, but now the house stinks! It STINKS, Jess! How can I have a party with the house STINKING!"

"Nikki, I'm a-scared. I want my daaad-dy! NOW!"

"I BEGGED Mom to let me have my party at the country club! Lyndsey's mom let her have _her_ party at the country club. But NOOO! Getting my mom to do anything these days is like pulling TEETH!"

WHY did MacKenzie have to say the _T_ word?!

Brianna totally lost it and started climbing out of the tub.

"OH, NO! Did you hear that! She's says she's going to pull out my TEETH! I wanna go hooome!"

"Brianna!! Wait . . . !" I tackled her and held her in a headlock. Finally, she stopped squirming and went limp.

Then the little brat BIT me!! HARD! I let go of her and yelped in pain like a wounded animal. "YEEOOOOW!" But I did it inside my head, so no one else heard it but me.

Brianna scrambled out of the tub, opened the bathroom door and disappeared into MacKenzie's bedroom!

I froze and held my breath. I could not believe this was happening to me.

Then I thought, maybe this is just a nightmare. Like those scary-weird dreams I was having earlier in the week about Chloe and Zoey. If I could just wake up, this would ALL go away.

So I closed my eyes, pinched myself really hard and tried to wake up.

But when I opened my eyes I was *still* standing in

MacKenzie's bathtub with Brianna's (now black-and-blue) teeth marks on my arm, next to a throbbing red pinch mark.

I SO wished I was DEAD!

Suddenly, another idea popped into my head. If I turned on MacKenzie's shower and stood under freezing cold water for an hour, I might die of pneumonia. But, even that could take a few days and I needed to be DEAD, RIGHT NOW!

"OMG! Jess, there's a little KID in my room! . . . How would I know? She appeared out of nowhere. I've told Amanda a million times my room is off-limits to her and her pesky little friends. Hold on . . ."

"MOM . . . !! Amanda and her friends are playing in my room again! Would you please do something . . . ?!"

"Okay, Jess, I'm back. If they so much as touch my makeup again, I swear, I'm going to strangle . . ."

"Don't you dare touch me you, you . . . WICKED

207

tooth fairy!" Brianna screamed at the top of her lungs.

Suddenly I felt really light-headed. I was sure I was about to faint.

"Hold on a minute, Jess . . ."

"WHO told you I was the tooth fairy? WHAT are you doing in my bedroom? And WHERE is Amanda?!!"

"You can't have my tooths! NEVER!" Brianna shouted bravely.

"MOM!! AMANDA!! Hold on, Jess. I have to get rid of this little kid. Then I'm going to KILL Amanda! Okay. Outta my room, right this—"

"STOP! Let go of me! I LOVE my tooths!"

There was a loud thump and MacKenzie shrieked.

"MOM! I've just been attacked by a demonic munchkin! OMG! I think I'm bruised! I can't wear my new

OOOW! YOU LITTLE...!

← BRIANNA BATTLING THE WICKED TOOTH FAIRY!

Jimmy Choo flip-flops with a big bruise on my leg!"

"Are you still there, Jess? I can't have my party like this. I've got a bruise the size of a pancake. NO! . . . I didn't get bruised *by* a pancake! I said . . . Hold on . . . !"

I could hear MacKenzie hobbling down the stairs like a one-legged pirate. Click-klunk, click-klunk, click-klunk.

"MOM! Last week Amanda and her friends put gum in my hair and coloured with my lipsticks! Now one of them just . . ."

When it sounded like MacKenzie's screeches were coming from a safe distance away, I jumped out of the bathtub, grabbed Brianna and tossed her over my shoulder like a sack of rotten potatoes.

Without stopping even once I hauled her down the stairs, through the hall, to the foyer and out the front door.

I deposited her butt in the backseat of the van and slammed the door.

My dad was in the back, loading up his equipment.

"Oh, there you girls are! Perfect timing. I'm all done."

As Dad started the van and drove off, I stared at the house, half expecting MacKenzie to come limping out the front door ranting that Brianna be arrested for creating a bruise that prevented

210

her from wearing her new Jimmy Choos at her birthday party. Amazingly, Brianna sat calmly in the backseat and seemed quite pleased with herself.

"Daddy, guess what? I went to use the bathroom, and after I washed my hands with strawberry soap and put on cupcake body spray, I saw the tooth fairy with rollers in her hair talking on a fairy phone and she said she was going to strangle me and pull out all of my teeth to make dentures for old people. So when she grabbed me I kicked her and she let go and started screaming for her mommy. Then she flew back to fairyland to go to a party for Jimmy Shoe. She's not so nice, that's for sure! I like Santa and the Easter Bunny much better."

Lucky for us, Dad was only half listening to Brianna's rambling. "Really, pumpkin? So is that what your *Princess Sugar Plum* movie was about?"

At the next stoplight I noticed a carload of teen

boys pointing and laughing. I put my plastic bag back over my head and slouched down in the seat.

I was so mad I could SPIT!

All of this drama for a measly ten bucks!!

I'm starting to get really excited because the avant-garde art competition is only eight days away! I decided to enter my watercolour painting that took me two whole summers at art camp to complete. I spent more than 130 hours on it.

The only complication is that I gave it to my mom and dad last spring for their sixteenth wedding anniversary. So it's technically not mine anymore. It was either my painting or spending my entire life savings of $109.21 to buy them dinner at a fancy restaurant.

But I knew the dinner was going to be a total rip-off, because I watch the Food Network. All of those five-star restaurants serve really gross stuff like frog legs and snails and then give you a tiny portion on a really big plate with chocolate syrup drizzled over it and a garnish. And "garnish" is just a fancy name for a plain old piece of parsley.

So, to save money, Brianna and I decided to cook

a romantic candlelit dinner for Mom and Dad as an anniversary surprise. We took a big bucket and a net to the pond at the park and hunted down some fresh frog legs and snails.

It was MY brilliant idea to make it an all-you-can-eat buffet, since we were basically getting the food for FREE.

CHEF NIKKI AND HER ASSISTANT PREPARE A TASTY GOURMET DINNER OF FROG LEGS AND SNAILS

ME PLAYING WITH MY FOOD

LOVE AT FIRST SIGHT

SAUCE →

RUNAWAY SNAIL

PARSLEY

FRESH FROG LEGS

FRESH SNAILS

Trying to prepare a gourmet dinner was definitely a lot harder than I thought it would be. The frogs kept jumping out of the bowl, and the snails wouldn't stay on the plate. Unfortunately, none of those shows on the Food Network explained how to control all the critters while you're trying to cook 'em.

And Brianna was no help WHATSOEVER! She was *supposed* to be my assistant, but she kept swiping the frogs and kissing them to see if they'd turn into princes. I scolded her really good about that because she had *NO IDEA* where those frogs' lips had been!

Not surprisingly, Brianna threw a big hissy fit when it came time to put the food in the oven. She said they were her friends and, "friends DON'T COOK friends!" I had to admit, she DID have a good point. So we decided to take Mom and Dad's anniversary dinner back to the pond and let them go. I guess you could say they were really lucky. "They" meaning the frogs and snails, not Mom and Dad.

Since our dinner plans fell through and I didn't

want to part with my life savings, I stuck a big red
Christmas bow on my watercolour painting and used
that as a gift instead. Mom and Dad must have
really loved it because they paid a ton of money
to have it professionally matted and put into an
expensive antique frame. Then they hung it in our
living room, right over the couch.

Even though it's now a priceless family heirloom
with tremendous sentimental value, Mom said I could
borrow it for the avant-garde art competition as
long as I took really good care of it.

I was like, "Mom, don't worry! Nothing's going to
happen. I'll be supercareful. I PROMISE!"

Although, now that I think about it, Jamie Lynn
Spears probably told her mom the exact same thing.
Hmmm . . .

I couldn't believe that MacKenzie actually came to school on crutches today. She even stuck little heart stickers on them so that they matched her new Gucci hobo handbag. Only someone as vain as MacKenzie would try to look CUTE while hobbling around on crutches. She didn't have a cast on her leg or anything. Just a SpongeBob Band-Aid below her left knee. HOW FAKE IS THAT?!!

According to the latest gossip, MacKenzie was taking scuba diving lessons on Saturday from this really hot ninth grader when she "ruptured her shin" while saving him from drowning. She supposedly did mouth-to-mouth resuscitation on him until the ambulance arrived. And since the poor guy's dying wish was for her to escort him to the hospital she was forced to cancel her birthday party. So she rescheduled it for Saturday, October 12th at her parents' country club. I was like, Yeah, RIGHT!

MacKenzie is such a LIAR and a DRAMA QUEEN! Why couldn't she just tell the truth and admit her

217

party was canceled because her house was infested with bugs and stank from bug spray?

Anyway, today I could hardly wait for lunch. Chloe and Zoey were even more excited than I was. We sat at our usual table and snarfed down our lunch as fast as we could.

Then I rolled up Zoey's sleeve, took out my lucky pen and got started on her tattoo. She kept giggling and squirming and saying it tickled. I said,

"LISTEN, ZOEY, SHUT UP AND SIT STILL OR I'M GONNA TURN ANY STRAY INK MARKS INTO UGLY BABY SNAKES!!"

218

Lucky for her, she stopped moving after that.

Practically everyone in the cafeteria was staring at us, but I ignored them and kept right on working. Zoey's tattoo turned out really cool and she loved it.

READING... AN EXTREME SPORT!

I was just getting started on Chloe's tattoo when the weirdest thing happened.

Jason Feldman got up, left the CCP table and sat down at OUR table to watch. He's just THE most popular guy in the entire school and president of the student council.

On the cuteness scale, I would say he was a 9.93 out of 10.

"You're doing a tattoo with a pen?! Cool! It looks so real. I should know because my brother just got one for his eighteenth birthday."

"It's our special LSA project for National Library Week," Chloe said and batted her eyelashes at him all flirtylike.

"Yeah! And all the latest fashion magazines say tattoos are HAWT!" Zoey added in this really nasally voice that sounded a lot like Paris Hilton.

Those two were acting so phony-baloney, it was sickening. I thought I was going to puke up my lunch right in Jason's lap.

"So what do I have to do to get one?" Jason asked excitedly. "Donate a book or something? Do you have a sign-up sheet?"

Zoey's and Chloe's faces lit up at the same time

220

and I could see the little lightbulb click on in their brains.

I just sighed and rolled my eyes. First it was the tattoo thing, then *Ballet of the Zombies* and then running away to live in the secret underground tunnels at the NYC public library.

I didn't know if I could put up with much more of this drama.

Chloe fluttered her eyelashes at Jason again. "Well, Nikki is art director, I'm overseeing book procurement and Zoey here handles scheduling. Zoey, would you please give Jason our sign-up sheet?"

"Er . . . what sign-up sheet?" Zoey asked, looking confused.

Chloe winked at her and said really loudly, "You know, the *SIGN-UP SHEET* in your *NOTEBOOK*, silly!"

Finally, Zoey caught on. "Oh, *THAT* sign-up sheet! Of course!" She gazed at Jason and giggled nervously.

Zoey whipped out her notebook, tore out a sheet of paper, scribbled TATTOO SIGN-UP SHEET across the top and handed it to Chloe.

Chloe added the words BOOK DONATION REQUIRED (NEW OR USED)!! in big bold letters and gave it to Jason.

I was shocked and appalled to see Chloe and Zoey lying like that. I always felt honesty was a very important quality in a friend.

Jason scrawled his name on the sign-up sheet and then yelled to his lunch table on the other side of the cafeteria, "Hey, Crenshaw! Get Thompson and come check this out."

Ryan Crenshaw was a 9.86 and Matt Thompson was a 9.98. They both came over and sat down at OUR table, right next to Jason.

Then the three of them started laughing and talking to me, Chloe and Zoey like we were CCP girls or something.

That's when I decided that, although an honest friend was nice, an "I-can-hook-you-up-with-really-cute-guys" friend was far better.

And besides, Chloe and Zoey weren't actually lying. They were just over-embellishing some fabricated truths.

Even though I was enjoying all of the unexpected attention there was an incessant gnawing deep down inside my gut that had me really worried.

WHY were the three most popular CCP guys suddenly sitting at a lunch table, flirting with Chloe, Zoey and me, the three biggest DORKS in the school?

And WHAT exactly did they want from us?

Then I had to force myself to ponder the most

INTRIGUING and TROUBLING question of all . . .

Was my lucky pen going
to MELT from all of
the CCP GUY
HOTNESS?!

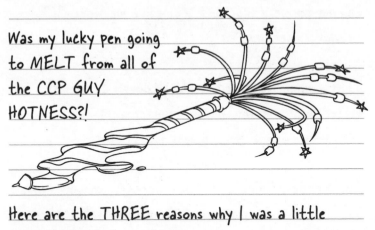

Here are the THREE reasons why I was a little
worried about my pen . . .

| JASON (The Prep) | RYAN (The Jock) | MATT (The Bad Boy) |

Within minutes seven more guys had crashed our
table and were passing around the sign-up sheet
and boasting about how wicked their tat was going
to be.

I finally finished up Chloe's tattoo, and she said it was perfect.

Jason rolled up his sleeve and took Chloe's place.

"Hey, dudes. Listen up! Mine is gonna say, 'GUITAR HERO'!!"

All of the guys started slapping him on the back and giving him high fives and fist bumps. He was acting all smug, like he was getting a new sports car or something.

Then a large crowd of girls gathered around the large crowd of guys to watch me work on Jason's tattoo.

"Isn't she the new girl?"

"I think her locker is right next to MacKenzie's."

"She's, like, *THE* best artist in the entire school."

"Hey, I wanna sign up! Give me the sheet next . . ."

"What's her name?"

"Mikki, Rikki or Vicki, I think."

"Whatever her name is, the girl's got SKILLZ."

"I'm SOOO jealous! I can't draw a stick figure."

"She's in my French class. Her name is Nikki Maxwell!"

"I'd LOVE to draw on Jason Feldman. He's HAWT!"

"OMG! I'd give ANYTHING to be Nikki Maxwell!"

I was starting to feel like a POP STAR!

The only CCPs not at our table were MacKenzie and her little group. They were GLARING at us from across the cafeteria.

By the end of lunch period I had completed seven tattoos, Chloe had collected nine books and Zoey had scheduled eleven people to get tattoos tomorrow at lunch.

We decided to call our new LSA project:

"Ink Exchange: Trade a Book for a Tattoo!"

In no time the ENTIRE school was gossiping about it.

Mrs Peach said collecting books for charity was
a wonderful idea and she was really proud of us.
Brandon even congratulated me and said he wanted
to interview me for the school newspaper on Friday
since I was "breaking news". He said he planned to
photograph a few students showing off their new
tattoos for the article. Now I can hardly wait for
Friday to get here ☺! There's a chance we might
actually become good friends.

But the absolute, most mind-blowing thing about all
of this is that Chloe, Zoey and I started the school
day as LSA DORKS and ended it as CCP DIVAS!

HOW COOL IS THAT?! ☺!!

	Today	Total
TATTOOS	17	24
BOOKS	34	43

This tattoo craze has really caught on at WCD!
I did eleven more during lunch and most of the
CCPs sat at our table to watch. It was pretty cool
hanging out with them and they were not mean or
snotty like we thought they'd be. I guess it was just
a matter of getting to know them better.

Surprisingly, I ended up doing another six tattoos
while I was on LSA duty. It seemed like everyone
and their mother was getting library passes during
fifth-hour homeroom and pestering me.

But Mrs Peach said she didn't mind me not shelving
books, since I was working on our group project.

So far, we've collected a total of forty-three books
for charity, which is fantastic. But it was mainly
because Chloe decided to start charging two books

per tattoo instead of one. Zoey and I thought one book was perfectly fine and we told her so.

But Chloe said that, since she was the director of book procurement, it was her decision, not ours, so it didn't matter what we thought. Now how RUDE was THAT?!

I was like, "Okay, Chloe! We're supposed to be doing this as a group project! Who DIED and made you QUEEN?!"

CHLOE THE GREAT, QUEEN OF BOOKS →

But I just said it in my head, so no one else heard it but me. So now we're getting TWO books for each tattoo, although it seems a bit GREEDY if you ask me. ☹!

WEDNESDAY, OCTOBER 2

	Today	Total
TATTOOS	19	43
BOOKS	57	100

I used to daydream about everyone at WCD knowing my name. And today more than two dozen people said hi to me before I even got to my first-hour class. It made me happy to have so many new friends ☺.

In biology we had to choose a lab partner and look at dust mites under a microscope. I thought for sure that Brandon was going to ask me to work with him. But three people interrupted him while he was trying to talk to me.

They were all like, "Hey, Nikki, let's work together so we can talk about my new tattoo design." But I didn't want to talk to people I hardly knew about tattoos. I wanted to have a really deep emo convo with Brandon about dust mites.

In the end I got stuck with Alexis Hamilton, the

captain of the cheerleaders. The whole time we were working all she did was blab about how they (the cheerleaders) needed me to come up with a "superhot" tattoo for their big game against Central, which, BTW, was on Friday.

But I already knew this because I overheard them talking about it in front of my locker this morning.

HEY...! WHERE'D SHE GO?!

A few of them were waiting around for me after second hour and they seemed pretty cranky. It wasn't like I was afraid of them or anything; I just jumped inside my locker because I can be a little shy at times.

ME BEING HUNTED DOWN BY AN ANGRY MOB OF CHEERLEADERS!

Anyway, I told Alexis that everyone had to sign up with Zoey first. But she said Zoey had a waiting list of 149 people through next Wednesday and she needed the tats right away since it was kind of an emergency. Alexis said she had already donated three books for each tattoo to Chloe, and Chloe was authorising the squad to be placed at the top of the waiting list.

So, NOW it was *THREE* books?!

I told Alexis that since Zoey was director of scheduling and Chloe was director of book procurement, she should probably just ignore Chloe. Then Alexis got an attitude about the whole thing and refused to talk to me or help write our lab report on dust mites. Talk about a cruddy lab partner!

But what really upset me was that Zoey had scheduled 149 people without asking me first. I have a French test on Friday and a geometry test next Monday and I'm barely pulling a C in each of those classes.

How am I supposed to study if I'm staying up past midnight EVERY night designing tats for all of these people?! And I haven't had time to eat lunch for the past two days!

Then, as I was leaving class, Samantha Gates stopped me to say how much she loved her tat of Justin Timberlake. She said all of her friends in the drama club wanted one too. She invited me to hang out with them after school on Friday and I told her I'd let her know. But how can I have a social life when I have to draw tattoos 24/7? ☹!

THURSDAY, OCTOBER 3

	Today	Total
TATTOOS	33	76
BOOKS	99	199

I had a really CRUDDY day today! It seems that all Chloe, Zoey and everyone cares about is TATTOOS.

I came to school early and did nine. Then I did fourteen at lunchtime and another ten during library. That's thirty-three tattoos!

Then I overheard Zoey tell Chloe, behind my back, that I worked "slower than a constipated snail in an ice storm," and I needed to speed up since she now had 216 people on the waiting list for next week. I was so NOT doing 216 tattoos in one week! And I told Zoey that right to her face. In a really friendly way.

Then Chloe wanted to know why I told Alexis to ignore her. She said that, since the cheerleaders had a big game, she thought they should be put at the top of the list for tomorrow. That's when Zoey said, as the director of scheduling, that the decision was hers alone and she didn't care *what* Chloe thought. Which was the EXACT same thing Chloe had said to us a few days ago.

Then Mrs Peach came over and asked us to PLEASE lower our voices because we were, after all, in a library.

But I knew better. It WASN'T a library . . . !

IT WAS A WICKED
TATTOO SWEATSHOP! ☹

ME
(feeling very
miserable) →

FRIDAY, OCTOBER 4

TATTOOS TODAY - A BIG FAT ZERO!

BOOKS TODAY - A BIG FAT ZERO!

WHY?

First of all Chloe and Zoey were mad because I didn't come to school early and they had seventeen people waiting for tattoos.

Well, excuuuuse me! But I had a French test today that I had to study for.

Then, at lunch, there were twenty-five people waiting. But instead of sitting at table 9 and helping me, Chloe and Zoey sat at the CCP table on the other side of the cafeteria.

I could see them giggling and acting all flirty with Jason, Ryan and Matt while I was supposed to be working my butt off like CINDERELLA or somebody!

But I nearly FREAKED when I saw MacKenzie give Chloe and Zoey INVITATIONS to her rescheduled party for next Saturday!

They were pink envelopes with big white satin ribbons tied around them, just like the one she had given ME.

And then taken back when she UNINVITED me!

Chloe and Zoey were acting all happy and sucking up to MacKenzie, even though they knew she HATED my guts.

SO I did the most mature and rational thing possible under the circumstances . . .

I QUIT ☹!

If I have to draw one more tattoo, I'm going to

VOMIT!

I thought Chloe and Zoey were my real friends.

238

But now I can see that they were just USING me all along to earn that trip to NYC for National Library Week.

HOW COULD THEY DO THIS TO ME?!

Then Brandon came up to my locker all smiley and said he wanted to interview me for the newspaper after school. But I told him to just forget it because my tattoo career was OVER! He asked me if I was okay and I said, "Yeah, it's all good! I just need to find some new friends." He just blinked and looked kinda confused. Then he shrugged and walked away.

So now it's like CHLOE, ZOEY and BRANDON are all TRIPPIN.'

I hope the three of them have a blast at MacKenzie's little party, since they all got invited and I DIDN'T!!

But it wasn't like I was jealous of them or anything. I mean, how totally juvenile would THAT be?!

239

I had the most horrible nightmare! It was like something out of the twilight zone.

MacKenzie was spitting bugs at me and all I could hear was the fifth-hour bell ringing and ringing.

IT WAS LIKE EVERYONE WAS OUT TO GET ME!!

Thank goodness I finally woke up. That's when

I realised it was morning and the telephone was ringing, not the fifth-hour bell. I dragged myself out of bed and answered the phone on my desk. It was my grandma calling to tell us she was planning to come visit us for two weeks at the end of the month. I told her my parents must already be out running errands or something since they hadn't answered the phone.

Then she asked me how I was doing and I told her not so good. I said I was thinking about transferring out of my school and asked her what she would do if she were me. She said it was NOT so much about the school I chose, but whether I chose to be a chicken or a champion.

Which, of course, had ABSOLUTELY NOTHING to do with ANYTHING! Since Grandma was talking out of her head again, I told her that I loved her, but that I had to go because someone was at the door. Then I hung up.

I wasn't lying to her because, unfortunately, Brianna and Miss Penelope were at my bedroom door. Miss

Penelope wanted me to watch her do a medley of songs from *High School Musical 3* in the stylings of Amy Winehouse.

I had been awake for less than three minutes and had already been forced to deal with my senile grandma, my hyperactive sister and a wacky puppet. I climbed back into bed, pulled the covers up over my head and SCREAMED for two whole minutes.

So many FREAKS and not enough CIRCUSES!!

PLEASE, PLEASE, PLEASE make all of this NOT really be happening to me. Today has been the WORST day of my ENTIRE life!!

It all started Sunday night when I was sitting at my desk doing review problems for my geometry test.

My mom came into my room around midnight to tell me she was leaving the house extra early in the morning to chaperone a field trip for Brianna's class.

"Nikki, since you have a test and the art competition tomorrow, it's REALLY important that you set your alarm clock so you don't oversleep in the morning."

I was like, "Thanks, Mom. Good night!"

I really did plan to set my clock. As soon as I finished my geometry problems.

But the next thing I knew, it was morning and I was

STILL sitting at my desk with my geometry book open.

I just about had a heart attack because, according to my clock, it was 7:36 a.m. on MONDAY, and my first-hour class started at 8:00 a.m.!

The only logical explanation was that I must have fallen asleep while studying at my desk.

ME GETTING MY SNOOZE ON

(AND DROOLING ALL OVER MY GEOMETRY BOOK)

My day was off to a very bad start!

I had overslept, I didn't have a ride to school, my painting needed to be turned in for the art show and my geometry test started in less than twenty-four, no, make that twenty-three, minutes.

Even the weather perfectly matched my miserable mood. It was dark, overcast and pouring rain.

I was fighting back my tears when suddenly I heard the low rumble of our garage door opening. I ran to my bedroom window and spotted the flicker of bright headlights.

IT WAS MY DAD ☺! And he was leaving the house.

I rushed around my room in a panic, trying to get dressed before he pulled out. I jumped into my jeans and slid on my jacket. When I couldn't find one of my shoes I decided to just change into my gym shoes once I got to school.

I grabbed my backpack and my painting and dashed

downstairs like a maniac. By the time I got out the front door my dad was already pulling into the street.

I ran down our driveway, waving my arms and screaming hysterically.

"Wait, Dad! Wait! I overslept! I need a ride to school!"

Only, I couldn't run very fast because I was loaded down with my backpack and the painting. Of course, my bunny slippers didn't help the situation either.

Unfortunately, my dad DIDN'T see me! ☹

So I just stood there in our driveway in the pouring rain feeling really, really cruddy. I couldn't believe I was going to miss the art show, receive an F on my geometry test and get an unexcused absence, all in the same day. I got this large, painful lump in my throat and I felt like crying again.

But my dad must have finally noticed me in his rearview mirror or something, because suddenly he slammed on his brakes. SKKKRREEEEEECCHH! I took off running down the street towards the van as fast as I could.

As I climbed in, Dad chuckled. "Does Sleeping Beauty need a ride to school, or are you waiting for your prince?!"

I ignored his corny little joke and collapsed into the backseat of the van. I was soaking wet, but I felt happy and relieved. All was not lost! Yet, anyway.

But I also felt really anxious. For the first time this year I was riding to school in the roachmobile!!

And if anyone saw me getting out of it I was going to absolutely DIE!

By the time we pulled up to the front of the school the rain had finally stopped. Thank goodness the only other vehicle around was a large truck with some men in uniform carrying in tall flat panels. I guessed that they were the displays for the art show.

I thanked Dad for the ride, grabbed my painting and climbed out of the van. Just as I was about to slam the door shut he waved and pointed to my backpack on the floor.

"Hey, I think you're forgetting something!"

I carefully set my painting on the ground and leaned it against the side of the van.

Then I climbed back in and grabbed my backpack.

"I think I'm all set now! Thanks again, Dad!"

I waved and slammed the van door shut.

I could NOT believe that I had actually made it to school in one piece with six minutes to spare. And not a single soul had spotted me getting out of the roachmobile, which was a miracle in and of itself.

Then I noticed a girl wearing matching Burberry raincoat, hat and boots climbing out of the back of the truck parked in front of us.

"Hey, careful with that, buddy! It's a piece of art, not a piece of plywood!" she snarled at one of the men.

I froze and thought about trying to duck back into the van to hide until she left. But it was too late!

MacKenzie's mouth dropped open.

At first she had a look of shock on her face as

she stared at me, my van and Max (yes, the roach).
Then her lips spread into a really evil grin.

"Wait a minute! YOU'RE the same Maxwell as
Maxwell's Bug Extermination?! And what is that
hideous brown thing on top of your van, a dead
horse?! Let me guess, it's supposed to be a matching
set with those two dead bunnies on your feet?!"

I just glared at her and didn't say a word.

Okay, MacKenzie was the undisputed winner if we
were competing for richest snob, cutest designer
wardrobe, most friends, coolest bedroom or biggest
house.

But, we WEREN'T.

Avant-garde art was all about pure, unadulterated
TALENT, which MacKenzie could NOT buy with her
parents' money.

It was her Fab-4-Ever fashion illustrations against
my watercolour . . .

And that was when I finally remembered my painting.
I spun around and lunged to grab it just as my dad
was pulling out.

But I was too late! I gasped and watched in horror
as the van tyre slowly crushed glass, antique wood
frame, my hopes and my dreams. It was shockingly
painful to see the unique expression of me that had
taken more than 130 hours to capture in watercolour
so brutally destroyed in a matter of seconds.

But the torn, twisted and splintered mess on

the side of the curb was not nearly as ugly as MacKenzie's final insult.

"Oh, no! Was that your little art project?! Too bad! Hey, just throw some bugs on it and enter it as a modern art piece called *Maxwell's Bugs on Garbage*."

Then she cackled like a witch and sashayed off. I just HATED when MacKenzie sashayed!

I watched sadly as the roachmobile turned the corner and disappeared down the road.

For the first time in my life, I wished I were inside it, warm and dry and speeding away. Away from MacKenzie. Away from friends who were really NOT my friends. Away from Westchester Country Day Middle School.

I didn't fit in at this place and I was sick and tired of trying. I sat down on the side of the curb, next to the pieces of my painting and cried. The rain started to pour again, but I didn't care.

I had been sitting there like forever, trying to sort things out inside my head, when I noticed it had stopped raining. On ME, anyway.

Then, I recognised that faint aroma of Snuggle fabric softener, Axe body spray and red licorice.

I looked up and was surprised and slightly embarrassed to see Brandon standing there holding an umbrella over me.

"You . . . okay?"

I didn't answer.

253

Then he extended his hand. I just looked at it and sighed. If I sat out on the curb in the cold rain much longer, I'd probably end up dying of pneumonia. Which, BTW, didn't sound like such a bad thing.

I grabbed hold of his hand and he slowly pulled me up off the wet curb.

I could NOT believe we were doing this stupid little scene all over again. How pathetic!

I rolled my eyes, sniffed and wiped my runny nose on the back of my hand. I was NOT going to let him see me cry.

Both of us just stood there not saying anything. He was staring at me and I was staring at the ground.

Suddenly, Brandon dug deep into his pocket and fished out a wrinkled-looking piece of tissue.

"Um . . . I think you have . . . something on your face?"

"Probably SNOT!" I said sarcastically and snatched the tissue from his hand.

"Yeah. Probably," he said, trying hard not to smile. "Like . . . I dig those shoes!"

"They're NOT shoes. They're bunny slippers! I was in a REALLY big hurry this morning, okay!"

I blew my nose at him loudly and angrily. HOOONKK!

"So . . . um, it looks like you had a little accident with your project."

"I wouldn't call it 'little'."

"Well, if it will make you feel any better, MacKenzie is entering some life-size paper dolls. I'd say your painting is STILL better than hers. Even in twenty-seven pieces. With mud smeared on it. And a few worms."

A mischievous grin slowly spread across Brandon's face.

255

"Come on. Everyone knows you have more talent in your smallest burp than—"

"Yeah! I know. I KNOW . . . !" I said, interrupting him and blushing uncontrollably. I HATED when he did that to me!

Okay, even though I was mad at the world, I had to admit, this whole thing was a little funny. In a really bent sort of way.

Finally, I smiled at Brandon and he winked at me. He was such a DORK! But in a good way. He had a slightly weird sense of humour and was friendly and a little shy ALL at the same time. And, unlike me, he didn't obsess about what other people thought about him. I think THAT was probably the coolest thing about him.

"Thanks for the umbrella!"

"Hey, no prob!"

Then we both walked to the front entrance.

Even though the building was warm, I felt really chilled.

My slippers were soaked and it seemed like I was wearing sponges dipped in ice water on my feet.

"I need to get my shoes out of my locker and then go to the office to call my dad. Hopefully, he can drop off some dry clothing."

"So . . . I'll walk you to the office, if you don't mind. My class is on the way."

As Brandon and I made our way down the hall, some people stopped and stared, while others pointed and laughed. But I just ignored them.

I knew I looked pretty crazy. With every step I took, my bunny slippers went *sloshie-squeak, sloshie-squeak, sloshie-sqeak* and left small puddles of water behind me.

When I finally got to my locker there was a large crowd of kids gathered around it. At first I thought they were there for tattoos, but everyone quickly scattered.

Then I saw what they were looking at.

It felt like someone had punched me in my stomach so hard, I could hardly breathe. I covered my mouth and tried to blink back my tears for what seemed like the tenth time this morning.

Someone had written on my locker in what appeared to be Ravishing Red-Hot Cinnamon Twist lip gloss.

Which, BTW, was MacKenzie's favourite.

"I—I'm really sorry!" Brandon stammered. "Only a real loser would do something as mean and stupid as . . ."

But I didn't hear the rest of what he said.

I turned around, pushed my way through the crowded hallway and went straight to the office to call my parents.

I couldn't take it anymore!

I was leaving Westchester Country Day Middle School.

And NEVER coming back!

Today I stayed home from school with a cold and just lounged in bed all day and drank lemon tea.

The Tyra Banks show rocked, as usual, but for some reason it didn't cheer me up.

After my dad picked me up from school yesterday, I started thinking that maybe I was overreacting.

Watching my painting being smashed into a zillion pieces had been pretty traumatic, but it was mainly MacKenzie who was making my life miserable.

Maybe WCD wasn't such a horrible place. Maybe if I tried talking to Chloe and Zoey, we could go back to being friends again. Maybe Brandon hadn't written me off as a total loser.

So, on Monday afternoon, I called the library desk during fifth hour to talk to Chloe and Zoey.

Plus, I was a teensy bit curious about how

MacKenzie's art project had turned out. Okay, I admit, I was DYING to know! My hands were trembling as I dialed the phone.

"Library front desk, Zoey speaking."

"Hi, Zoey, it's me, Nikki. I was just calling to see how you guys are doing. You'd NEVER believe what happened to me this morning."

Then I heard Chloe's muffled voice in the background.

"OMG! It's her?! Just say you can't talk right now because we're really busy. We don't have time to waste."

"Um . . . what's up, Nikki? Brandon told us everything that happened. Actually, he's here right now. Too bad about your art project . . . ," Zoey stammered nervously.

"Yeah, I know. So, what are the three of you do—"

"Listen, Nikki, I really have to hang up now. We're really busy with, um . . . a project. Chloe and Brandon said hi."

"Wait, Zoey! I just wanted to—"

"Sorry, gotta go. See you tomorrow. Bye."

CLICK!

After that conversation, there was no doubt in my mind that Chloe, Zoey and Brandon practically hated me. So there wasn't really anything left to do but make plans to transfer to a new school.

And have a really good CRY.

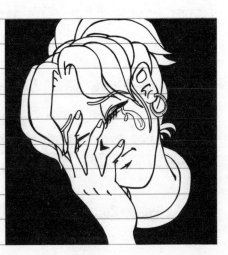

Which is what I've been doing on and off for the past twenty-four hours.

The only good thing

that's come out of all of this is that my parents have been so worried about my emotional state, they've finally agreed to let me transfer to the nearby public school.

I thanked my dad for arranging the scholarship and all, but unfortunately it just hadn't worked out.

Surprisingly, Mom and Dad took the news about their anniversary painting being destroyed really well.

I even promised I would paint them a new one, although Brianna insisted that she wanted to do it instead.

"Don't worry, Mom and Dad! I'm almost done making you a brand-new anniversary present and it's way better than Nikki's dumb ol' painting!"

But I had a really bad feeling about Brianna's art project.

When I asked her if she had used finger paints or crayons, she said, "Nope! A black permanent marker.

And I drew it over the couch in the exact same spot where your painting was hanging!"

Brianna said her drawing was called . . .

THE MAXWELL FAMILY VISITS PRINCESS SUGAR PLUM ON BABY UNICORN ISLAND

When Mom saw Brianna's wall mural she just about fainted. And then Brianna tried to get out of it by blaming Miss Penelope.

It was kind of nice to laugh again after feeling so hopelessly depressed.

My parents and I drove over to WCD forty-five minutes early so we could get everything taken care of before the students started arriving.

As Mom and Dad sat in the office chatting with the secretary and completing the school-transfer paperwork, I couldn't help noticing the colourful displays off the main entryway for the art competition.

No matter how much I tried to convince myself I didn't care, I just HAD to know if MacKenzie had won. It was like I was obsessed or something.

If I hurried I could stop by the art competition for a few minutes and still have time to clean out my locker, get back to the office and be out of the building before anyone spotted me.

"Well, I better get going," I muttered to my parents. I grabbed the empty cardboard box I had brought to carry the junk from my locker and headed down the hall.

The art exhibit was set up in the large student lounge near the cafeteria and was divided by grades. I hurried past the sixth- and seventh-grade displays to the eighth-grade section. There were about 24 entries and I immediately spotted MacKenzie's.

Like everything she did, it was big, bold and over the top. She had painted seven life-size mannequins dressed in her Fab-4-Ever fashions on six-foot-tall panels.

I had to admit she was actually a pretty good fashion illustrator.

But the strange thing was that I didn't see her first-place ribbon.

Although, knowing MacKenzie, she probably had already taken it home so her parents could have it bronzed to match her baby shoes.

Then again, maybe NOT.

I was surprised to see the blue ribbon was hanging on the very last display.

I couldn't help pitying the poor artist who would have to put up with the drama over MacKenzie's very public and humiliating defeat.

The winning display was a series of sixteen 8 x 10 close-up black-and-white photographs of inked artwork.

When I read the title and artist's name, I almost

FREAKED OUT!

THE STUDENT BODY
BY NIKKI MAXWELL

I immediately recognised my tattoo artwork on Zoey's shoulder, Chloe's arm, Tyler's neck, Sophia's ankle, Matt's wrist and on and on.

So _this_ must have been the "project" Chloe, Zoey and Brandon were working on when they said they were too busy to talk to me on the telephone Monday afternoon.

Slowly, but surely, the reality of the situation started to soak in.

I was like, "OMG! I WON first place in AVANT-GARDE ART! FIRST PLACE and five hundred dollars!"

Thanks to Chloe, Zoey and Brandon! They must have cooked up this elaborate scheme after my painting got destroyed. And that fantabulous display with MY name on it had probably taken hours to complete.

I was SO wrong about them. They were the BEST friends EVER! And more than a dozen other kids had volunteered to be photographed. All of this totally BLEW MY MIND!

Maybe WCD was not such a horrible place after all. I actually had real friends here. And of course it didn't hurt that I was now rich, rich, rich beyond my wildest dreams!

I hurried back to the office in a daze and burst inside.

"Mom, Dad! I've changed my mind. I want to stay!"

They both looked surprised.

"Honey, are you okay?" my mom asked, concerned.

"Actually, Mom, I'm GREAT! I've changed my mind. I want to stay. PLEASE!"

"Well, it's up to you. Are you sure?" my dad said, putting down his pen.

"I'm sure. I'm REALLY sure!"

The secretary gathered the papers from my dad, ripped them in half, and tossed them into the wastebasket.

"This is great news!" She beamed. "And congratulations on your first place in the art show! You're coming to the reception for the winners this Saturday, right? They'll be giving out the cash awards and the catered dinner is fabulous."

My parents looked totally confused. "I thought you said you didn't—" my mom began, but I quickly interrupted her.

"Listen, I'll explain all of this later. Like, don't you both have somewhere to be?" I smiled and waved good-bye to them, hoping they would take the hint and get lost.

Mom kissed my forehead. "Okay, hon! We're glad you've decided to hang in there."

"Yeah, and you can thank Maxwell's Extermination for hooking you up!" my dad said and winked. "I knew it would work out for you here if you just gave it a chance."

"Well, I gotta go! Oh. Here, Dad!" I tossed him the cardboard box. "Can you get rid of this for me?"

Then I turned and rushed out of the office.

Students were starting to fill up the halls and a few actually congratulated me. As I made my way back to my locker I wasn't quite sure what to expect, but I was ready and willing to deal with it.

The graffiti had been cleaned up, thank goodness. But there was something new on my locker.

I knocked on the door of the janitor closet and then peeked inside.

Nikki,
Please meet us in the janitor's closet ASAP!
It's very, very important!

Chloe and Zoey

271

Chloe and Zoey were sitting on the floor in a corner and looking pretty sad. I felt kind of sorry for them.

"We owe you an apology for the way we acted," Chloe said. "We got really carried away with all of the tattoo and book stuff. And that wasn't fair to you."

"Yeah! And we learned who our real friends are too. The CCPs wanted to hang out with us as long as you were doing the tattoos. What a bunch of phonies!" Zoey added.

"Actually, I kind of figured that out too. That angry mob of cheerleaders was too scary!" I said, shuddering at the memory.

"Listen, please don't be mad, Nikki!" Chloe said, starting to tear up. "But we have a confession to make . . ."

Zoey cleared her throat.

"Well, after we heard about the accident with your

painting we rounded up the kids with your best tattoo artwork and Brandon took pictures of them during lunch. Then he printed out the photographs on the computer in the newspaper office. Mrs Peach let the three of us work on your entry the entire afternoon in the library. We called it *The Student Body*."

"And you'll never guess what happened," Chloe sniffed, blinking back tears.

"I won!"

"YOU WON!!" they said together.

"Wait! You KNEW?!" Zoey asked, surprised.

"Yeah. I just found out a few minutes ago."

"We know we shouldn't have done it without asking you first. But there wasn't time. You're not mad at us, are you?" Chloe asked, and gave me jazz hands to try to lighten the mood.

"Actually, I am. I'm VERY ANGRY!" I hissed. Chloe and

Zoey both hung their heads and stared at the floor.

"We're sorry. We were just trying to help . . ."
Zoey muttered.

"You're supposed to be my friends. How could
you two do this to me? I'm so TICKED! I would
have given ANYTHING to have seen the look on
MacKenzie's face when she LOST!" I was trying so
hard not to laugh that I was starting to snort.

At first both girls blinked and looked bewildered.
Then, slowly, smiles spread across their faces until
they were grinning from ear to ear.

"OMG! Nikki, you should have seen her," Chloe
squealed. "When they announced you as the winner
she went into shock!"

"It was hilarious! MacKenzie threw a hissy fit right
there in front of the judges!" Zoey snickered.

Pretty soon we were laughing and joking in the
janitor's closest just like old times.

"Uh-oh! I think I just heard the first bell," I groaned.

"Let's get out of here before we start smelling like a mildewy mop!"

Chloe and Zoey opened the door and then stood there waiting for me to leave first.

"Talent before . . . brains!" Zoey winked and then gave me the stink eye.

"Talent before . . . beauty!" Chloe grinned and then gave me jazz hands.

"Hey, girlfriends, I see the talent! But, other than me, there's definitely no brains or beauty up in here!" I teased.

That's when Chloe and Zoey both socked me on my arm. "OW!!" I giggled. "That hurt!!"

There must have been a big sale at the mall yesterday or something, because four girls were wearing the exact same outfit.

I hadn't really noticed it until I overheard MacKenzie ridiculing them in the hall.

"OMG! Look at that! They're ALL wearing the same butt-ugly ensemble! Wait, don't tell me. They were giving them away for free with a purchase of a McDonald's Happy Meal!"

It was only 7:45 a.m., and I was already visualising tape over her mouth.

When MacKenzie finally noticed me she tried to act all innocent.

"Just in case you're wondering, I DIDN'T write 'Bug Girl' on your locker. Lots of people wear Ravishing Red-Hot Cinnamon Twist, you know."

I just rolled my eyes at her. That girl is SUCH a liar! I didn't believe her for one second.

MacKenzie flipped her hair and gazed at her perfect image in her mirror.

"Besides, even if I did it, you don't have any proof!"

Then she applied her morning layer of lip gloss.

Since I was stuck having a locker next to MacKenzie's for the rest of the year, I decided to utilise the mind-over-matter coping strategy that Zoey had developed.

In my MIND I was so OVER being impressed with MacKenzie, because she didn't MATTER!

Although, I have to admit, those hoop earrings she was wearing were to die for.

Why is it that huge dangly earrings look really GLAMTASTIC on the CCP girls? But when normal girls (like me) wear them, we end up needing reconstructive cosmetic surgery.

POPULAR GIRL IN
BIG DANGLY EARRINGS

UNPOPULAR GIRL IN
BIG DANGLY EARRINGS

Zoey, Chloe and I sat together at lunch at table 9 and a lot of people stopped by to ask about tattoos. Since our Ink Exchange Program was such a big hit and we had already collected almost two hundred books for charity, we decided to continue it for just three days each month, starting in November. It was going to be great NOT having to hide inside my locker between classes due to my fear of angry mobs — I mean, my shyness.

But the strangest thing was that I was actually starting to look forward to attending National Library Week at the NYC public library. And we had a good chance of being selected. I mean, just think about it! Chloe, Zoey and me in Manhattan for five days without our 'rents! How EXCITING would THAT be?!

We were going to have Friends, Fun, Fashion, Food & Flirting like it says in *That's So Hot!* magazine. And maybe even get tickets to the

TYRA BANKS SHOW!

I just LOVE that GIRL!!

I also planned to take full advantage of the "Meet-n-Greet" with all those famous authors. I had no idea an autographed novel was so valuable.

I planned to collect a half dozen and then sell them on eBay for big bucks. Then, KA-CHING!! I could buy that iPhone I've been wanting! Am I NOT brilliant?! ☺!

BTW, I decided to save the $500 prize money for art camp next summer. It was going to be my fifth year attending and my instructor said I already had an art portfolio strong enough for college. Which is pretty fantastic seeing as I'm not even in high school yet! She said if I continued to work really hard I could maybe land a four-year scholarship to a major university. *SWEET!*

Brandon stopped by our table to ask if he could interview me about winning the avant-garde art competition, since it was "breaking news".

I thanked him for taking the photographs of my tattoo designs and told him what a great job he had done on them. But he said it was no biggie and he planned to use the photos for the article he was writing.

Then MacKenzie came over, acting all friendly, and actually congratulated me. I was so shocked, I almost puked my lunch on her Jimmy Choos!

But I think she really just wanted to flirt with Brandon, because she kept batting her eyes at him all fluttery, like she had accidentally stuck a false eyelash to her eyeball or something.

How does she have the nerve to do that right to my face?! Probably because she has the IQ of lint.

In spite of the fact that we had agreed not to do any tattoos until next month, Chloe and Zoey insisted that I do just ONE more . . .

FOR MYSELF.

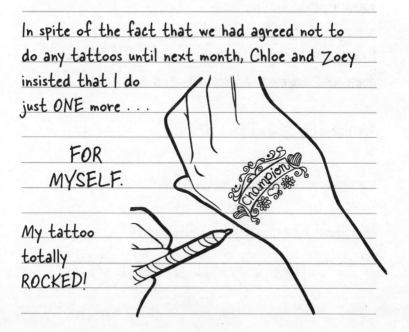

Champion!

My tattoo totally ROCKED!

Okay, I admit I was wrong about Grandma being senile. But I was correct about that DEMENTED puppet, Miss Penelope.

After lunch was over Brandon walked with me to biology class. He brushed the hair out of his eyes with his fingers (again) and smiled at me kind of shylike.

"So I . . . um . . . was wondering if . . . um . . . you wanted to be lab partners for 'structure of mitochondria'?"

I could NOT believe he asked me that. So I looked deep into his eyes, all serious, and said:

"WHEEEEEEEEEEEEEEEEEE!!"

I'm sure he thought I was CRAZY.

But, hey! I can only be myself, right?

I'M SUCH A DORK!
☺!!!

Recipe for disaster:

Take four parties.

Add two friends and one crush.

Sprinkle one mean girl out to RUIN Nikki's life.

Mix well, put fingers over eyes and CRINGE!

Turn the page to find out what happens

next to Nikki in

Party Time

FRIDAY, OCTOBER 11

I can't believe this is happening to me!

I'm in the girls' bathroom **FREAKING OUT!!**

There's NO WAY I'm going to survive middle school.

I've just made a complete FOOL of myself in front of my secret crush. AGAIN ☹!!

And if that wasn't bad enough, I'm still stuck with a locker right next to MacKenzie Hollister's ☹!

Who, BTW, is the most popular girl at Westchester Country Day Middle School and a total SNOB. Calling her a "mean girl" is an understatement.

She's a KILLER SHARK in sparkly nail polish, designer jeans and platform Skechers.

But for some reason, everyone ADORES her.

MacKenzie and I do NOT get along. I'm guessing it's probably due to the fact that she

HATES MY GUTS 😞!!

She is forever gossiping behind my back and saying supermean stuff like that I have no fashion sense whatsoever and that our school mascot, Larry the Lizard, wears cuter clothes than I do.

Which might actually be true. But STILL!

I do NOT appreciate that girl BLABBING about my personal business.

This morning she was even more vicious than usual.

OMG, NIKKI!! Could you please go write in that diary somewhere else?! Your hideous green shirt is clashing with my new lip gloss flavour and it's giving me a MIGRAINE!

ME

I could NOT believe she actually said that to me!

I mean, how can a COLOUR clash with a FLAVOUR?!
DUH!! They're, like, two TOTALLY different,
um. . . THINGS!

That's when I lost it and yelled, "Sorry, MacKenzie!
But I'm REALLY busy right now. Can I IGNORE you
some other time?!"

But I just said it inside my head, so no one else
heard it but me.

And if all of that isn't enough TORTURE, the
annual WCD Halloween dance is in three weeks!

It's the biggest event of the fall, and everyone is
already gossiping about who's going with who.

I'd just totally DIE if my secret crush

BRANDON

asked me to go!

Yesterday he actually asked ME to be his lab partner for biology class!

I was SO excited, I did my Snoopy "happy dance".

La, La, La!
I'M . . .

La, La, La!
SO . . .

La, La, La!
HAPPY!!

And today I had a sneaking suspicion Brandon was going to "pop the question" about the Halloween dance.

The school day seemed to drag on FOREVER.

By the time I got to biology class, I was a nervous wreck.

Suddenly, a very troubling question popped into my head and I started to panic: what if Brandon only thought of me as a lab partner and nothing more?!

That's when I decided to try to impress him with my charm, wit and intelligence.

I gave him a big smile and went right to work drawing all these teeny-tiny lint-looking thingies I saw under the microscope.

Biology Lab *3   Oct. 11

Microscope Observations

Out of the corner of my eye, I could see Brandon staring at me with this urgent, yet very perplexed, look on his face.

It was obvious he wanted to talk to me about something SUPERserious. . . ☺!

Those thingies in the microscope really WERE just LINT! OMG!! I was SO EMBARRASSED!!

I knew right then and there I had pretty much blown any chance of Brandon asking me to the dance.

But the good news was, I had made a startling scientific discovery about the biogenetics of my intelligence and even reduced it to a working formula.

MY IQ ≤

Then things got even WORSE.

Dirty gym → sock

I was in the girls' bathroom when I overheard MacKenzie bragging to her friends that she was practically almost 99.9% sure she and Brandon were going to the dance together as Edward and Bella from *Twilight*.

I was VERY disappointed, but not the least bit surprised. I mean, WHY would Brandon ask a total DORK like ME when he could go with a CCP (Cute, Cool & Popular) girl like MacKenzie?

And get this! As they were leaving, MacKenzie giggled and said she was buying a new lip gloss JUST for Brandon. I knew what THAT meant.

I was SO frustrated and angry at myself.

I waited until the bathroom was empty, and then I had a really good SCREAM.

ME →

Which, for some strange reason, always makes me feel a lot better ☺.

Middle school can be very TRAUMATIZING, that's for sure!!

But the most important thing to remember is this: always remain CALM and try to handle your personal problems in a PRIVATE and MATURE manner.

ME, HAVING A PRIVATE SCREAM-FEST!

294

SATURDAY, OCTOBER 12

Today has been the MOST exciting day EVER!

I still can't believe I actually won first place and a $500 cash prize in our school's avant-garde art competition ☺!

Last week, without even telling me, Chloe, Zoey and Brandon entered photos of the tattoo designs I had drawn for kids at school.

So I totally freaked out when I found out I had won! Who would have thunk I'd beat out MacKenzie's awesome fashion illustrations?

And boy, was she ticked! Especially after bragging to everyone that she was going to win.

I can't wait to get my hands on all that money.

I had originally planned to use it to buy a mobile phone. But I decided it would be more prudent to save it for art camp next summer.

I'm investing in my dream of becoming an artist so I can spend all day curled up in bed in my fave pj's, drawing in my sketchbook and actually get paid for it. SWEET ☺!

Although, it would be kinda cool to use the money to fix up my very drab locker.

Adding a little bling would guarantee me a spot in the CCP clique.

ME, → showing off my awesome locker!

← iPod stereo system

← colour TV + computer monitor combo

← VCR/DVD player

ATM MACHINE

← personal ATM

Anyway, practically the entire school was at the avant-garde art awards banquet today.

I was very shocked when MacKenzie came over and gave me a big hug.

I think she only did it to make a good impression, because what she said to me was not very sportsmanlike at all.

"Nikki! Congratulations on winning first place, hon! If I had known the art show judges wanted talentless junk, I would have framed my poodle's vomit stains and entered it as abstract art."

OMG! I couldn't believe she said that right to my face.

She should have just scribbled

"I'M SO JEALOUS!!"

across her forehead with a black marker. That probably would have been LESS obvious.

I was like, "Thanks, MacKenzie. You're such a big BABY. So cry me a river, build yourself a bridge and GET OVER IT!"

But I just said it inside my head, so no one else heard it but me. Mainly because I'm basically a nice person and I don't like negative vibes.

It had absolutely nothing to do with me being a little intimidated by her or anything.

Chloe and Zoey sat right next to me during dinner.

And as usual, we were acting really silly and having random giggle attacks.

When Brandon came over to take a picture of me for the school newspaper and yearbook, I thought I was going to DIE!

He suggested that we go to the atrium across the hall, where the lighting was better.

At first I was happy that Chloe and Zoey wanted to tag along, because I was supernervous.

But the entire time he was snapping pictures, they

were standing right behind him making kissy faces at me and acting all lovesick.

OMG! It was SO EMBARRASSING!!

ZOEY

CHLOE

I was so angry I wanted to grab them both by their necks and squeeze until their little heads exploded.

But instead, I just gritted my teeth and prayed
Brandon didn't notice them goofing around behind
his back like that.

Chloe and Zoey are really nice and sweet friends,
but sometimes I feel more like their babysitter than
their BFF.

Lucky for me, when they heard that dessert was
being served, they rushed back to the banquet to pig
out some more.

Which meant Brandon and I were all alone!

Only it was kind of uncomfortable and a little embarrassing because instead of talking, we just stared at each other and then the floor and then each other and then the floor and then each other and then the floor.

And this went on for what seemed like FOREVER!!

Then FINALLY he brushed his shaggy bangs out of his eyes and smiled at me kind of shylike. "I told you you were going to win. Congratulations!"

I gazed into his eyes, and my heart started to pound so loudly my toes were actually vibrating. Kind of like standing near a car blasting your favourite song, but with the windows rolled up. And you can't really hear the melody part, but your innermost soul can feel the vibrations from the bass part going *Thumpity-thump!! Thumpity-thump!!*

And my stomach felt all fluttery, like it was being

302

attacked by a huge swarm of very. . . ferocious. . . yet fragile. . . butterflies.

I immediately realised I was suffering from a relapse of RCS (Roller-Coaster Syndrome).

I clenched my teeth and mustered every ounce of strength in my entire body to keep myself from gleefully shouting, WHEEEEEEEEEEEEEEEE!!

But instead, I uttered something far, far worse.

"Thanks, Brandon. Um. . . have you tried those cute little barbecued

303

wing-dings? They're actually quite delicious!"

"Did you just say. . . wing-dings?!"

"Yep. They're at the front table right near the punch. They also have honey glazed and hot-'n'-spicy. But the barbecued ones are my favourite."

"Um. . . actually, no! I haven't tried them."

"Well, you really should. . ."

"So, I. . . um. . . want to ask you something. . ."

"About the wing-dings?"

Brandon's face was intensely serious.

"No. Actually, I want to know if. . . you. . ."

I was holding my breath and hanging on to his every word.

". . . I mean, it would be totally cool if you would—"

"BRANDON!! There you are!! OMG! I've been looking for you everywhere!"

MacKenzie barged into the room and lunged straight for Brandon like an NFL linebacker trying to recover a fumbled ball.

"As the official school photographer, you really need to get a picture of me posing with my Fab-4-Ever fashion illustrations. They're about to take down my display!"

Then she just stood there smiling at Brandon all GOOGLY-EYED, twirling her hair around her finger.

Which was obviously a DESPERATE attempt to HYPNOTIZE him into doing her EVIL bidding.

"Brandon, please hurry! Before it's too late!" she whined breathlessly while glaring at me in total disgust like I was this huge pimple that had suddenly popped out on her nose or something.

305

Brandon rolled his eyes, sighed and gave me this very goofy but cute smile.

"So. . . we'll talk later, Nikki. Okay?"

"Sure. See ya."

As I walked back to the awards banquet, I felt very light-headed and a little nauseous.

But in a really GOOD way!

More than anything, I was now totally consumed with a burning curiosity.

Brandon had been about to ask me something really important when MacKenzie had rudely interrupted him.

Which left me with one very obvious and compelling question:

WHY AM I SUCH AN IDIOT?!!

Wing-dings?! I could NOT believe I had rambled on and on about the variety of delicious wing-ding flavours!

No wonder he didn't ask me to the dance.

At least my picture came out okay.

Brandon is such an AWESOME photographer!

I'm in the most HORRIBLE mood right now! I'm SO totally dreading school tomorrow.

If I hear one more girl mention that stupid dance, I'm going to SCREAM!! I keep hoping someone will ask me, but I know it's NOT going to happen.

What I need is a MAGIC love potion or something!

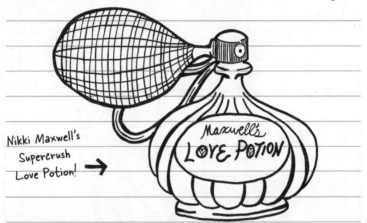

Nikki Maxwell's Supercrush Love Potion! →

Maxwell's LOVE POTION

I would definitely use it on Brandon because that's the ONLY way he'd ever like a LOSER like me.

Then I'd share it with girls all over the world who are suffering from the same problem.

Just one spray and your crush will fall madly in love with the first person he lays eyes on!

SUPERCRUSH LOVE POTION!
NOW EVERY GIRL CAN LIVE HAPPILY EVER
AFTER WITH THE GUY OF HER DREAMS!

Or maybe. . . NOT!!

My life is HOPELESS!! ☹!!

Tonight Mom and my little sister, Brianna, were putting up decorations for Halloween.

I knew what was coming next because it happens every single year.

Brianna sneaks up on everyone and tries to scare us with this big stupid-looking plastic spider.

It's almost like a Maxwell family Halloween tradition or something. Mom and Dad always put on this big act and pretend to be superscared just to humour her. And, of course, Brianna gets a really big kick out of it.

Personally, I don't think it's healthy to encourage her like that. What's going to happen when she gets older and starts attending middle school?

Hey! I already KNOW what's going to happen!

Brianna's going to take that plastic spider to school and shake it at people because she thinks it's appropriate behaviour.

And everyone at her school will think she's NUTZ!

Then I'll have to go through all the trouble of changing my last name so no one will know she's my sister.

My parents need to realise that raising an impressionable child like Brianna is a big responsibility.

Anyway, I was up in my room studying for my French test.

I was feeling a little grumpy because I was having a hard time remembering which nouns in French are masculine versus feminine.

Sure enough, Brianna showed up just like I expected:

I TOTALLY FREAKED!!

And that poor spider seemed a little traumatised too.

Brianna thought the whole thing was SO funny.

HA HA HA, Brianna!!

I don't know HOW I thought that real spider was Brianna's fake one.

Hers is purple with little pink hearts on it and is wearing high top sneakers and a big cheesy smile. It looks like the type of spider you'd find living in a Barbie Dream House or hanging out with SpongeBob SquarePants.

After that experience, I'll never forget that "spider" in French is *araignée*.

But, is it a masculine noun OR a feminine noun?!

OH, CRUD!!

I'm SO going to FLUNK this stupid test ☹!!

When I arrived at school this morning, I was surprised to see a note on my locker door from Chloe and Zoey:

NIKK!,

GUESS WHO'S GOING TO THE HALLOWEEN DANCE?! MEET US IN

THE JANITOR'S CLOSET ASAP!!

CHLOE & ZOEY

The janitor's closet is our secret hangout.

We meet there to discuss very important PRIVATE and HIGHLY CONFIDENTIAL personal stuff.

As soon as I stepped inside, I could tell Chloe and Zoey were superexcited.

"Guess who's going to the Halloween dance?!!" Zoey giggled happily.

"Um. . . I dunno. WHO?" I asked.

I was pretty darn sure it WASN'T one of us. We were the three biggest dorks in the entire school.

"SURPRISE!! WE ARE!!" Chloe screamed, jumping up and down and giving me jazz hands.

"And we've already arranged for three guys to be our dates! Sort of!" Zoey squealed.

"Sort of? What do you mean by 'sort of'?" I asked.

I was already starting to get a really bad feeling about this guy thing.

That's when Chloe and Zoey explained their crazy

plan for how we were going to snag really cool dates for the Halloween dance.

All in just five easy steps:

STEP 1: We sign up to be volunteers for the Halloween dance clean-up crew.

STEP 2: We arrive at the dance half an hour early, pretending like we're there to inspect for cleanliness. But instead, we secretly change into our fabulous costumes.

STEP 3: We quickly spread the rumour that the three cutest guys onstage with the band are our dates (even though they're really NOT).

STEP 4: Since the band is going to be busy performing the ENTIRE night, the three of us will dance, eat and hang out with one another.

STEP 5: We'll have FUN, FUN, FUN while everyone (including the CCPs) RAVES about our SUPERcute, SUPERtalented, SUPER-pop-star dates.

This plan was *ALMOST* as bizarre as the one where they were going to run away and live in the secret underground tunnels of the New York City Public Library.

I told them there was a slight chance their phony "My date's a band member!" scheme might work.

But it would mostly depend on what the guys in the band actually looked like.

CUTE 'N' MOODY MUSIC LOVERS . . .

Everyone would ENVY us ☺!

Everyone would LAUGH at us ☹!

The dangerous part is that this whole thing could easily backfire and ruin our reputations.

And the three of us already have a pretty pathetic ranking in the WCD CCP Popularity Index.

Here is a chart of the most UNPOPULAR people in our entire school.

WCD CCP POPULARITY INDEX

NINE MOST UNPOPULAR

ME
↓

1. Violet Baker
2. Theodore L. Swagmire III
3. Zoey Franklin
4. Janitor
5. Chloe Garcia
6. Head Lunch Lady
7. Larry the Lizard (school mascot)
8. Nikki Maxwell
9. Black Slime Mold (growing in locker room shower)

Since there would be a substantial risk I could end up more UNPOPULAR than black slime mold, we definitely needed to come up with a way better idea.

I suggested that we each make an inexpensive yet creative costume by taking a big green rubbish bag and stuffing it full of newspaper and going as. . . (drumroll please). . .

BAGS OF RUBBISH!!

How CUTE would that be?!

Especially if we were members of the clean-up crew.

We'd also need a pair of those yellow rubber gloves.

Just thinking about all the germy things that could be lying around after a big party like that actually made me shudder.

Ewwww!

And since we didn't have dates, we could spend the entire night doing Broadway-style dance numbers using a broom, mop and vacuum cleaner as our dance partners.

I personally thought my plan was pure GENIUS!

Us rocking it at the dance as. . .

THE CLEANING CREW!

But Chloe and Zoey were like, "Um. . . no offence, Nikki, but your idea is actually kind of. . . LAME."

Of course that little comment really ticked me off.

"Okay, girlfriends! You wanna know what I think is LAME?! LAME is attending the Halloween dance as the clean-up crew and then LYING to everyone that the band members are our dates!"

Chloe and Zoey got really quiet and just stood there staring at me with these big sad puppy-dog eyes.

And of course I felt kind of sorry for them because I personally knew what it was like to very desperately want to attend the dance.

So, being the sensitive and caring friend that I am, I decided to put aside my personal feelings and sign up for the Halloween dance clean-up crew.

I considered it a small sacrifice that would ultimately nurture true and lasting friendships.

The sign-up sheets for the Halloween dance committees were posted on the bulletin board right outside the office door.

Luckily for us, no one had signed up for the clean-up crew yet.

The thing that really bothered me though was the sign-up sheet for CHAIRPERSON of the Halloween dance committees.

SIGN-UP SHEET
HALLOWEEN DANCE
CHAIRPERSON*

~~Ryan Crenshaw~~
~~Diane Wane~~
~~Christina Hughes~~
~~Paige Clark~~
Violet Baker
THEODORE L. SWAGMIRE III
MacKenzie Hollister

*TO BE SELECTED BY STUDENT COUNCIL

For some reason, most of the people who had signed up had crossed their names off the list.

Which meant there were only three candidates for that position ☹!

PLEASE, PLEASE, PLEASE

let Violet Baker or Theodore L. Swagmire III be selected as chairperson.

Otherwise, this clean-up crew thing was going to turn into my worst

NIGHTMARE!

TUESDAY, OCTOBER 15

I LOVE fifth hour because Chloe, Zoey and I get to work as library shelving assistants (LSAs) ☺!

Some kids think the library is a quiet and boring place where only dorks and nerds hang out, but we always have a BLAST!

WE PUT BOOKS BACK ON THE SHELVES.

And our librarian, Mrs Peach, is supernice. On Fridays she bakes us these humongous double chocolate chip cookies with walnuts. Yummy!

I was a little surprised when Mrs Peach gave me a note saying I was supposed to report to the office immediately.

My parents were there waiting for me. They were picking me up from school early because they wanted me to attend the funeral of a Mr Wilbur Roach, a local retired businessman and former president of the Westchester Exterminators Association.

I couldn't believe that was actually his REAL name! Poor guy!

My parents and I had never met him. But since exterminators from all over the state were going to be there with their families, Dad thought it might be a good idea if we attended too.

I was like, JUST GREAT ☹!! And as if that wasn't bad enough, I had to listen to Dad's

Pure Disco 3 CD the whole drive there and back.

By the time I'd heard the song "Shake Your Groove Thing" for the thirty-ninth consecutive time, I wanted to jump out of the car window into oncoming traffic.

It goes, "Shake your groove thing, shake your groove thing, yeah, yeah," and then you just repeat those words 1,962 times until the song is over.

The whole experience ended up being very traumatic for me. I was also upset because I had a bad case of hiccups. Extremely loud ones.

During the memorial service, Mom kept giving me this dirty look like I was hiccupping on purpose or something. But I honestly couldn't help it.

And this guy named Mr Hubert Dinkle got really choked up while he was up there giving the eulogy. Mom said it was because Wilbur Roach was his best friend.

I think my hiccups must have got on his nerves or something because he stopped right in the middle of his speech, gave me the evil eye and growled.

I am so NOT lying. He actually growled at me!

My hiccups were driving everyone nuts.

I was waiting for Wilbur Roach to sit up and YELL at me too!

Although, THAT would have totally freaked me out! Mainly because he was supposed to be, like, you know. . . DEAD!!!!

Anyway, my hiccups kept getting worse. Then
Mr Dinkle got an attitude and acted pretty
RUDE about the whole thing.

After Mr Dinkle practically SCARED me to death AND made me drink that big glass of water in front of everyone, my hiccups *finally* stopped! Which was a good thing ☺!

I always wondered why they kept a pitcher of water up there next to the podium like that.

Who would have thunk it was for an emergency cure for a case of hiccups?!

After all the drama at that funeral, I'm pretty sure Mom and Dad won't be dragging me to another one anytime soon.

Thank goodness for that!

My only worry now is that since Mr Dinkle is superold and a part-time church organist, I might unexpectedly run into him again at some point in the future.

And then he'll give me a REALLY hard time for ruining his speech.

OMG!

I have NEVER laughed so hard in my entire life!

My mom got up extra early this morning and tried out some homemade beauty treatments and relaxation techniques that she'd seen on television.

She was wearing an oatmeal face mask with cucumbers on her eyes. And she had turned off all the lights in the family room to meditate on the meaning of her life.

That's what she said she was doing, anyway. Although, it looked to me like she was sitting in the chair snoozing.

Anyway, Dad walked in and turned on the lights and like

TOTALLY FREAKED!

EEEEEKKK!!

His scream was so loud and high-pitched, I thought it was going to shatter that big window in our family room.

Then, when Mom woke up and heard Dad screaming like that, she totally panicked and grabbed hold of him.

Which made him scream even LOUDER!

339

I guess Dad must have thought he was being attacked by some kind of oatmeal-crusted, cucumber-eyed zombie wearing a pink fuzzy robe with a bath towel wrapped around its head.

Which, I have to admit, DOES sound awfully scary when you think about it.

I only wish I could have caught that moment on video. I bet it would have got, like, 10 million views on YouTube.

Then some producer would have paid us a million dollars to do our own cheesy reality show.

OMG! I'm still laughing so hard my stomach hurts!

☺!!!

BTW, I have a really bad feeling about Chloe, Zoey and me being on that clean-up crew.

WHY?

Because when I got to school, everyone was buzzing about the student council selecting MACKENZIE to be the chairperson of our Halloween dance!

JUST CRAPTASTIC ☹!!

Of course she made a big fat hairy deal out of the whole thing.

She actually wore a special outfit for the occasion and insisted that everyone address her as "Miss Chairperson."

I personally thought the tiara and roses were a bit much.

It's not like I was jealous of her or anything.

Like, how juvenile would that be?

The first thing MacKenzie did was call an emergency meeting during lunch.

Only, there wasn't any type of REAL emergency that I could see.

Thirty of us just sat there in this huge auditorium listening to her make a ridiculous speech:

"I just wanted to congratulate my wonderful Halloween dance committee members and share with all of you my extraordinary vision for what will be the most spectacular event our school has ever experienced. In keeping with this goal, I am officially inviting each and every one of you to my very own birthday party. Which, BTW, has been rescheduled again for Saturday, October nineteenth, due to a conflict with the art awards banquet. I proudly extend this opportunity in hopes that a few of you more, um. . . shall we say. . . socially challenged individuals might experience firsthand what a glamourous and exciting party is like."

I almost fell out of my seat!

I could not believe MacKenzie had just called me socially challenged right in front of everyone, AND invited me to her BIRTHDAY PARTY!!!

Like, WHY would she want ME at her party?!

MacKenzie's speech went on for another ten minutes and when she finally finished, all the CCPs gave her a standing ovation.

MacKenzie said the committees for set-up, entertainment, publicity, decorations and food would meet daily starting tomorrow.

But the clean-up crew - which, BTW, was me, Chloe, Zoey, Violet Baker and Theodore L. Swagmire III - didn't need any meetings "because it doesn't take a brain to clean up."

It was very obvious to me that MacKenzie was treating us clean-up crew members like second-class citizens and I didn't like it one bit.

I personally felt it was of vital importance that we meet at least once to plan our cleaning strategy.

Next she encouraged everyone to come up with really creative Halloween costumes.

EXCEPT, of course, the clean-up crew. MacKenzie showed everyone sketches of the "supercute" uniform she had personally designed for us to wear the entire night.

OUR CLEAN-UP CREW OUTFITS DESIGNED BY MACKENZIE

It looked like a twist between a spacesuit and flannel underwear and came with four-inch platform boots.

FRONT

She said we could easily store twenty kilos of trash in each of the two large pockets in the front.

And if we had to go to the bathroom, we could simply

344

unbutton the large flap in
the back.

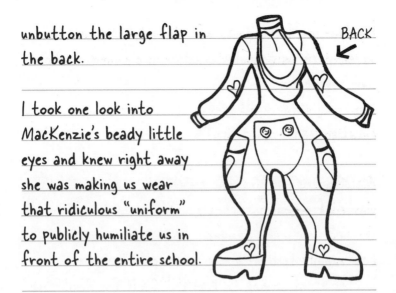

BACK

I took one look into
MacKenzie's beady little
eyes and knew right away
she was making us wear
that ridiculous "uniform"
to publicly humiliate us in
front of the entire school.

But she just smiled and batted her eyelashes all
innocent like.

After the meeting was finally over, I told Chloe
and Zoey there was NO WAY IN HECK I was going
to allow that girl to embarrass us like that.

But they were so excited about the possibility of
going to the dance that they didn't even care.

They told me I should try a little harder to be
more of a team player and give MacKenzie's uniform
a chance.

Because, even though it was absolutely hideous on paper, once we actually tried on the outfit it might look supercute.

I was so mad I could SPIT!

MacKenzie's meeting was a TOTAL and MASSIVE waste of my time.

I personally felt my lunch hour would have been better spent trying to KEEP DOWN the Tuna Fish/ Meat Loaf Casserole Leftover Surprise!

Brianna had a ballet recital this evening. I wanted to stay home and do my homework, but Mom said I had to go.

Every year it's exactly the same thing: cutesy little girls dressed up in cutesy little costumes, doing cutesy little dance routines to cutesy little songs.

Brianna didn't want to go to the recital either.

Mainly because she HATED ballet!!

Whenever Mom dragged her off to lessons, she would whine, "Moooommm! I wanna be a karate-chop girl! Not one of those pointy-toe-hoppers with the pink scratchy skirts!"

But since Mom had dreamed of taking ballet lessons when she was a little girl, she felt the next best thing was to give birth to a daughter and force HER to do it instead!

When I was younger, Mom tried to enroll me in a ballet class too.

Only after she dropped me off, I went straight to the girls' bathroom and ditched my leotard and ballet flats and changed into more appropriate dance attire. The COOL kind they wear on MTV.

Even though I was superexcited about dancing, my ballet teacher sent me home with a note:

Madame FuFu's
School of Dance

WE TURN CLUMSY, UGLY DUCKLINGS INTO
BEAUTIFUL, GRACEFUL SWANS.

Dear _Mrs Maxwell_ :

I have carefully evaluated the dance skills of

your daughter, _Nikki_ , and I suggest the

following placement:

____ BEGINNING BALLET CLASS

____ BEGINNING JAZZ CLASS

____ BEGINNING TAP CLASS

_X_ OTHER: Professional backup

dancer for pop star or rapper.

Good luck!

Sincerely,

Madame FuFu

Madame FuFu

I thought this was great news, but mom was pretty
much heartbroken I wasn't going to be a ballerina.

Unfortunately, Madame FuFu didn't like Brianna all that much either.

She was always sending her home early for disrupting the dance class.

And just last week Brianna got in trouble for defacing ballet school property.

Instead of simply apologising to Madame FuFu,
Brianna lied about the whole thing.

She was like, "But, Mommy! My friend Miss Penelope
wrote on that stupid ballet poster! Not ME!"

That was her story and she was sticking to it.

But everyone knows Miss Penelope
is actually Brianna's OWN hand
with a face doodled on it.

Everyone except
Brianna.

It's quite obvious to me my kid sister has some serious mental issues. I'm just sayin'. . . !!

Overall, the recital went okay. Except for the last dance number, called "Fairies and Flower Friends Have Fabulous Fun."

Brianna just stood there on the stage shivering, with this terrified look on her face. I felt kind of sorry for her.

Brianna

Although, I have to admit, it was partly my fault.

Brianna has this thing about the tooth fairy. She's been scared to death of her ever since I told her the tooth fairy took teeth from little children and Super Glued them together to make dentures for old people.

THE TOOTH FAIRY GLUING TEETH
TO MAKE DENTURES

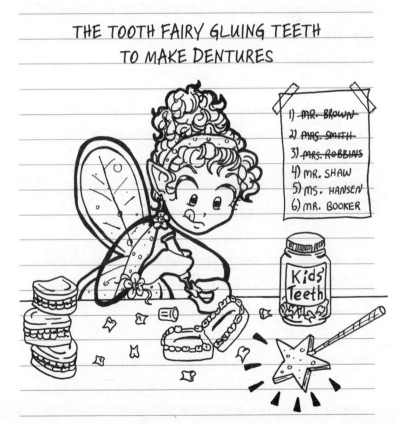

1) MR. BROWN
2) MRS. SMITH
3) MRS. ROBBINS
4) MR. SHAW
5) MS. HANSEN
6) MR. BOOKER

Kids' Teeth

I totally meant it as just an innocent little joke.

But now she's too afraid to go to the bathroom by herself at night.

Anyway, after the recital was over, we were getting ready to leave when Mrs Clarissa Hargrove, one of the ballet moms, came over and gave Brianna an invitation to a Halloween party for the ballet class.

She said it was going to be held at the Westchester Zoo in the Children's Petting Zoo building.

I was a little surprised when Mrs Hargrove congratulated me on my art award.

She said she was desperately looking for an artist to paint faces for the ballet party and was wondering if I would be interested.

Apparently, her niece, who also attends WCD, told her I was the best artist in the entire school and suggested that she ask me to help out.

And GET THIS!

Mrs Hargrove offered me $150 to paint faces and help with games for a couple of hours.

I was like, "Well, um. . . HECK YEAH!! ☺!!"

For $150, I would have painted her ENTIRE house. Inside and out!

It's not like I was going to be doing anything important on Halloween night anyway.

Except maybe cleaning up after the Halloween dance.

And now I had a really good excuse for NOT doing that phony "My date's a band member!" thing with Chloe and Zoey.

Mrs Hargrove said she would buy the paint and brushes and drop everything off next week.

So now I'm sitting in my room staring at a cheque for $150.

I can't believe I FINALLY have the money to get that phone I've been wanting.

I'm still obsessing over what Brandon wanted to ask me that night at the awards banquet.

According to MacKenzie (and all the latest gossip), he already has a date for the Halloween dance.

So the only other thing I can think of is that maybe he still wants to interview me about winning the art show since he asked me about it nine days ago.

Whenever I see him in class, he just says hi and bye and that's pretty much it. He's definitely a lot quieter than he used to be.

Or maybe he just doesn't want to be seen in public talking to a big DORK like me ☹!

MacKenzie doesn't help things either. Every time she sees Brandon and me near each other, she rushes over and tries to flirt with him by twirling her hair. She's been doing this ALL week. I definitely think she's up to something, but I don't know what.

I finally mentioned the whole Brandon thing to Chloe and Zoey while we were putting away books.

Chloe, who, BTW, is an expert on guy stuff, said I should simply ask him what he wanted.

I told her I had already tried to do that. But it was really difficult to talk to him during class with MacKenzie always butting in.

And if I asked him to meet me in the janitor's closet for a little privacy, he would think I was a WEIRDO.

Chloe and Zoey agreed with me 100%. Not about it being hard to talk to Brandon during class, but about him thinking I was a weirdo.

Then Zoey said she had overheard MacKenzie bragging in gym class that the editor of the school newspaper had assigned Brandon to cover her birthday party as a personal favour.

That's when Chloe said, "Hey, I have an idea! If

Brandon is going to be at MacKenzie's party, why don't you just talk to him there? It'll only take a few minutes and then you can leave."

"Are you KA-RAY-ZEE?!" I screamed. "There is no way in HECK I'm going to a party by myself with MacKenzie and all those CCPs!!"

That's when Chloe got this big sly grin on her face and started doing jazz hands!

I was like, UH-OH!! Not another of her WACKY ideas?!!

"Nikki, you're not going there ALONE! Because WE'RE coming with you!" Chloe shouted excitedly.

I could NOT believe Chloe and Zoey both volunteered to go with me to MacKenzie's party!

They said it was for moral support and because they're my BFFs.

And NOT because they wanted to have fun, dance,

or flirt with their secret crushes, Jason and Ryan, who, BTW, might ask them to the Halloween dance.

NOPE! We all agreed that MacKenzie's party was going to be strictly BUSINESS!

I had originally planned to use the $150 cheque from Mrs Hargrove to buy a new phone.

But when I checked my clothes, the only superfancy party dress I owned was from second grade and had buttons and bows all over it.

And I wouldn't be caught dead wearing that plain old dress from the awards banquet.

So I decided to use my phone money to buy a glamourous, designer, semiformal dress to wear to MacKenzie's party.

And for once my mom actually agreed to take me to the MALL instead of our usual discount department stores!!

I was like, YES ☺!!

While Mom helped Brianna shop for a Halloween costume, I went from store to store trying on the most fabulous dresses. I even found shoes, jewellery and other cool stuff to match each one.

I actually felt like I was doing a photo shoot for *America's Next Top Model*! All I needed was for Tyra Banks to suddenly appear.

She'd smile at me and another model very warmly and say, "I hold two photos in my hand. But only

ONE of you can continue in this competition. The ugly, lazy girl gotta pack and go home, y'all."

OMG! I just LOVE that girl ☺! I think she's a wonderful role model for teens.

Anyway, I had a BLAST trying on all those clothes!

WACKO
EMO

DRAMA
QUEEN
MEAN

BAGGY
SHABBY
CHIC

RAGING
REBEL
ROCKER

GOTH
GIRL
GROOVY

VERY
SCARY
VAMPY

363

COS GIRL
CUTIE →

← SILLY
CELEBUTANT

Unfortunately, none of these styles reflected the real and true me.

The mall was going to close in less than an hour and I was starting to panic. If I didn't find a dress, I couldn't go to MacKenzie's party.

Suddenly . . .

THERE IT WAS!!

But the only dress in my size was on this very
snotty-looking mannequin in the window.

So I rushed over to this very snobby-looking sales
clerk and tapped her on the shoulder and said,

"Excuse me, ma'am. But I absolutely LOVE that dress in the window! Could you please take it off the mannequin?"

But she was very busy putting out a very colourful display of toe socks.

And I'm guessing she did NOT want to be disturbed, because she just glared at me and said, "Young lady, can't you see I'm busy? Now SHOO! Before I call security!"

I was totally shocked by her totally inappropriate behaviour!

I even considered lodging a complaint with the manager since this was supposed to be an exclusive store for upscale customers.

Like, WHO in their right mind would even want to buy a pair of toe socks?!

I'm just saying. . .

Anyway, I really, really LOVED that dress!

And there was no way I was leaving that store without it.

So I decided to sneak inside the window display and take the dress off that mannequin myself.

I mean, how hard could it be?

Lucky for me, the only other person around was a little old lady browsing the support tights.

Things were going really well until I accidentally knocked her over and her head popped right off.

Not the little old lady's head, the mannequin's.

I was like, "Oh, CRUD!"

Every time I tried to stand her up, she would just teeter back and forth and fall right over again. And her head would roll across the floor like a bowling ball.

To make matters worse, a crowd of people had gathered around the window and were staring at me.

And this toddler was crying really loud because that headless mannequin must have looked pretty dang scary.

Anyway, after what seemed like forever, I finally got that mannequin to stand up. I also found a new outfit for her to wear.

Then I paid for the dress and got the heck out of there.

Before that mean sales clerk called security and had me arrested me for vandalising the window display.

Believe me, I WON'T be shopping at that swanky department store anytime soon.

OMG! I can't believe what just happened to me at MacKenzie's party. I have never been so humiliated in my entire life ☹!

Her party was at a ritzy country club and looked like something straight out of that MTV show *My Super Sweet 16*.

A humongous room had been converted into a dance club, complete with a stage, a DJ and strobe lights.

And to really make things upscale, a private chef was preparing sushi and freshly baked pizza while a Starbucks barista served mocha Frappucinos, caramel lattes and strawberry-banana Vivanno smoothies.

All the guys were decked out in suits and ties and the girls were wearing party dresses by all the most famous designers.

There must have been two hundred kids there, and everyone was dancing and having fun.

I was like, WOW!!

Chloe and Zoey looked FANTASTIC! And they said I looked like a glamourous Hollywood celebutant.

The three of us felt supernervous and totally out of place being there with all those CCP kids.

We placed our presents for MacKenzie on an overflowing gift table and then tried to act coolly nonchalant.

You know, like we really WEREN'T dorks and it really WASN'T the first and ONLY middle school party we'd ever been invited to.

But Zoey kind of messed up our "very cool party girl" cover.

Suddenly her eyes widened to the size of golf balls and she let out a high-pitched "SQUEE!"

On a nearby table was this huge chocolate fountain.

It had a fancy crystal platter piled high with an assortment of fresh cut fruit for dipping into the warm chocolate.

The three of us practically ran over to take a closer look.

It was the most AWESOME thing ever!!

And while we were standing there, the strangest thing happened.

Jason and Ryan walked right up to Chloe and Zoey and asked them to dance!!!

The three of us just froze and went into total shock.

I thought for sure we were going to need one of those defibrillator thingies that medics use when people have heart attacks.

Chloe and Zoey just stood there blinking, with their mouths dangling open, like deer caught in headlights or something.

They looked at me and then the guys, then back at me, then at the guys, then back at me and then at the guys again. This went on, like, forever!

Finally, I spoke up.

"Actually, they'd LOVE to dance!"

That's when Chloe and Zoey started blushing profusely.

"Um. . . sure!" Zoey squeaked.

"Okay, I guess!" Chloe giggled.

Then they both squeezed my arm. And because I'm their BFF, I knew just what they were thinking.

That maybe the guys were going to ask them to the Halloween dance.

I kind of winked and said, "Hey! Go right ahead! I'm going to try this yummy chocolate fountain. Have fun, 'kay?"

Chloe and Zoey smiled nervously as the four of them made their way to the crowded dance floor.

I was SO happy for them.

I couldn't make up my mind which fruit I wanted to try first — strawberry, apple, pineapple, banana or kiwi. However, since it was free, I just piled a few of each on my plate and then drizzled warm chocolate over the whole thing. I couldn't wait to dig in!

It was hard to believe I was actually enjoying myself at MacKenzie's party. If only I could find Brandon and *finally* get to talk to him about that interview or whatever, it would be a PERFECT night.

I was a little surprised when MacKenzie and her BFF, Jessica, walked up to me and started talking.

"OMG! I can't believe you actually came!" MacKenzie said, smiling at me. "And your dress and shoes are supercute! Wait, don't tell me. You raided lost and found?!"

I gritted my teeth, took a deep breath and then plastered a fake smile on my face.

"Happy birthday, MacKenzie! And thanks for inviting me!"

I didn't want to waste any of my energy dealing with her drama. The ONLY reason I had come to her stupid party was to talk to Brandon.

Suddenly Jessica stared at me and then scowled.

377

"OMG! What's that on your fruit? Eww!"

"What?!" I looked down at it, expecting to see a bug or a hair or something stuck in the chocolate.

"THAT! Don't you see it? GROSS!" she exclaimed, pointing and frowning like she saw something slimy with eighteen legs.

I brought my plate up for a closer look.

"What? I don't see any—"

But before I could finish my sentence, Jessica slapped the bottom of my plate.

WHACK!

As the plate went airborne, a few stray pieces of fruit landed in the chocolate fountain with a *kerplunk*, splashing chocolate on my face.

However, the vast majority of the gooey mess landed on the front of my dress in chunks and stuck there.

I froze and stared at it all in HORROR!

My beautiful designer dress was totally ruined!

MacKenzie and Jessica doubled over in laughter and a half dozen other CCP girls joined in.

"I am SO sorry, Nikki! It was totally an accident!" Jessica sneered.

"OMG, Nikki! You should have seen the look on your face!!" MacKenzie shrieked.

"It looks like you were in a food fight. And LOST!" Jessica snorted.

The lump in my throat was so large I could barely breathe. Tears filled my eyes and I tried to blink them away. I didn't want to give MacKenzie and Jessica the pleasure of seeing me cry.

I grabbed some napkins and wiped my dress until all that remained was a large, faint brown stain.

It suddenly became very clear that the only reason MacKenzie had invited me to her party was to publicly humiliate me.

And, like an idiot, I had taken the bait. How could I have been so STUPID?! I didn't care about talking to Brandon anymore. I just wanted to go home.

Suddenly, MacKenzie gasped and whipped out her lip gloss. "OMG! Jess, isn't that the photographer from the Westchester Society Page? I think it's time for our close-up!"

That's when I noticed that the fountain was vibrating and making a strange gurgling sound.

I guessed that the pieces of fruit that had dropped inside were clogging things up or something.

"What a beautiful fountain! Let's get a shot with the birthday girl and her best friend standing right beside it," the photographer guy said as he dunked a huge strawberry into the chocolate and popped it into his mouth.

Okay, I had a really bad feeling about their taking a photo for the Westchester Society Page right next to that fountain.

Mainly because it was making a low rumbling noise that sounded like a twist between a clogged-up garbage disposal and a plugged-up toilet.

It was NOT a happy sound. I was outta there!

I admit, that big smudge on my dress looked bad.

But MacKenzie and Jessica looked like they'd been mud wrestling in a vat of chocolate fudge and then tried to clean up by showering in chocolate syrup.

Which, BTW, made me feel a whole lot better ☺.

I wrapped my shawl over my dress and then hurried to the front desk in the lobby to call my parents.

I decided not to tell Chloe and Zoey I was leaving.

They were still dancing with Jason and Ryan and seemed to be having a really great time.

And if they were lucky and landed "real" dates for the Halloween dance, they wouldn't have to do that phony "My date's a band member!" thing.

I was standing outside the main door, waiting for my parents and trying to ignore a really bad headache, when I heard a familiar voice.

"Hey, are you leaving already?"

It was Brandon. Just great ☹!!

I adjusted my shawl to make sure that stain wasn't showing and just stared straight ahead.

"Yeah, I am. Actually, I don't even know why I came."

"I'm outta here too. I just needed shots for the newspaper."

384

"Um. . . that's nice, I guess," I said, trying to muster a smile.

Our eyes met, but I quickly looked away. We both just stood there not saying anything.

I kept fiddling with my shawl, but out of the corner of my eye I could see him staring at me.

"Are you okay?"

"Yep. Just supertired."

"I'm sorry to hear that. . ."

"Oh! Here's my dad. See ya."

I rushed to the curb to meet the car as it pulled into the U-shaped driveway.

"Hey, wait a minute, Nikki! I just—"

Without looking back, I opened the car door and collapsed into the backseat.

I was exhausted, angry, humiliated and confused.

And to make matters worse, I think I was having my first migraine.

More than anything, I just didn't have the energy to chitchat with Brandon right then.

As my dad pulled away, I peeked into the rearview mirror.

Under the glare of the street light, I could see him just standing there in the middle of the street with his hands in his pockets and a hurt look on his face.

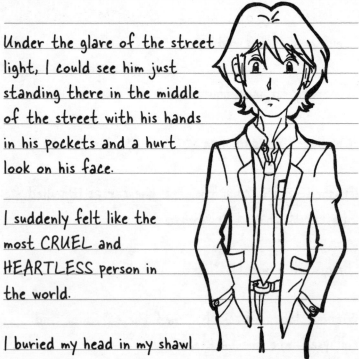

I suddenly felt like the most CRUEL and HEARTLESS person in the world.

I buried my head in my shawl

and had a really good cry right there in the backseat.

WHY was I acting so crazy?

WHY was everything so confusing?

WHY was I hurting a person I really cared about?

It was just another DREADFUL day in the PATHETIC life of a not-so-popular party girl ☹!

When I woke up this morning, I was in a decent mood.

For about thirty seconds.

Then all the HORRIBLE memories from MacKenzie's party came flooding into my brain like a massive tidal wave.

I just wanted to crawl deep under the covers and hide there for the rest of the school year.

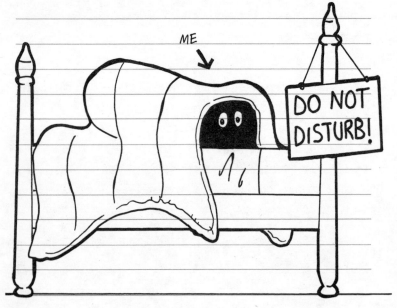

ME

DO NOT DISTURB!

Now I'm feeling hopelessly depressed ☹.

I checked my answering machine and was not that surprised to see Chloe and Zoey had each left me, like, a dozen messages.

But I decided NOT to call them back. The last thing I felt like doing was blabbing on the phone for three hours about how MacKenzie and Jessica had tortured me and destroyed my dress.

Although, I can't blame Chloe and Zoey for being supermad at me for just disappearing into thin air like that.

I'd wanted to get the heck out of there as fast as possible. I guess I completely BUGGED OUT!

Anyway, around noon my mom came bouncing up the stairs to tell me that lunch was ready. Then out of the blue she smiled really big and said, "Guess what, honey?! I have a little surprise for you!"

ME, TRYING TO GUESS WHAT'S IN THE BOX

And NO. I DIDN'T think she had finally got me a mobile phone. Even though I've been wanting one, like, FOREVER!

Apparently, Dad was sorting through stuff in the attic when he discovered a box of Mom's old costumes from her Shakespeare theater days back in college.

When she showed me her Juliet costume, I was like, WOW!

The dress was made of the most beautiful plush purple velvet and had gold embroidered trim along the sleeves and skirt.

It came with a curly wig and a fancy eye mask decorated with purple beads, ribbons and feathers.

The outfit looked like something a real princess might wear. And it was in great condition, even after being in storage all those years.

Because the dress had a lace-up front, Mom thought it would fit me perfectly. She said I was welcome to use it for the Halloween dance.

I thanked her and told her it was the best costume ever.

But when she begged me to try it on, I kind of stammered and came up with the excuse that I had to study for a big test. I promised her I would try it on after dinner.

Which, BTW, was a lie. I absolutely LOVED the costume.

But I had no intention of wearing it.

EVER!

After last night's disaster, just the thought of attending another party actually made me want to. . . VOMIT!

I guess I'm still traumatised or something.

At this point, I plan to skip the Halloween dance and just help out at Brianna's ballet party. I've already spent the money I was

392

paid, so I'm pretty much STUCK doing that one.

But I'm not going to stress out about it. I mean, what could possibly go wrong at a party for a bunch of six-year-olds?!

I'll be spending the rest of Halloween night sitting on my bed in my pyjamas, staring at the wall and sulking.

Which, for some reason, always makes me feel better ☺.

I just hope Chloe and Zoey don't get mad at me and decide they don't want to hang out with me anymore.

Having friends is SO complicated!

Which, BTW, reminds me that I am NOT looking forward to seeing Brandon in biology class tomorrow.

That look on his face just keeps haunting me.

I feel really awful about acting the way I did, but I couldn't help it.

I'm pretty sure by now he

HATES MY GUTS!!

If I was him, I definitely would. ☹!!

All day MacKenzie and Jessica have been giving me the evil eye and whispering about me.

I'm so sick of them, I could just SCREAM!

Apparently, they're mad at me for that whole chocolate fountain fiasco.

And MacKenzie's spreading the rumour that I only came to her party to try to humiliate her so Brandon wouldn't want to take her to the dance.

This whole thing was THEIR fault!

If Jessica hadn't smacked my plate like that, those little pieces of fruit wouldn't have fallen into the fountain and made it malfunction.

I can't stand MacKenzie, but I'd NEVER try to mess up her birthday party.

I mean, how immature would THAT be?!

Even though I hadn't seen Chloe and Zoey since the party, they must have heard all the gossip.

I wasn't surprised to see they'd left a note on my locker.

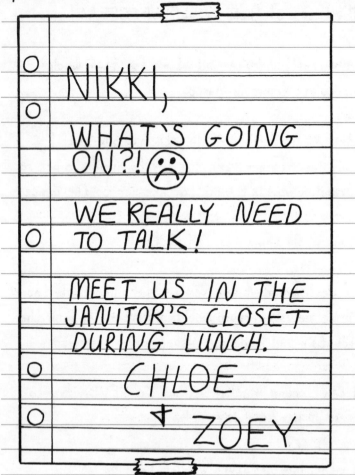

I had no choice but to come clean and give them all the nitty-gritty details about what had happened and why I'd left the party early.

Only, I didn't mention the part about Brandon since I was still confused about all that.

I was TOTALLY surprised when Chloe and Zoey got SUPERangry.

Not at me, but at MacKenzie and Jessica.

They said they'd suspected something bad had happened to me after I left so suddenly without telling them.

They hugged me and said they were really sorry I'd had to go through all that alone.

Of course, that just made me cry.

So Chloe, Zoey and I had a really good group cry.

It was Chloe's idea that the three of us resign from the clean-up crew. And Zoey totally agreed.

They said we were NOT going to tolerate MacKenzie and Jessica's bullying any longer.

I couldn't believe my ears! I knew Chloe and Zoey had their hearts set on attending the dance as the clean-up crew and doing that phony "My date's a band member!" thing.

Unless, of course, Jason or Ryan ask them to go, which they haven't. . . yet.

But they said it was no biggie. And even though the three of us wouldn't be going to the Halloween dance this year, there was always next year.

I could NOT believe that my wonderful BFFs would make such a HUGE sacrifice just for ME!

I got this huge lump in my throat and I wanted to cry all over again.

Zoey composed a letter stating that we were resigning from the clean-up crew and the three of us signed it.

Then we gave the letter to Jessica, since MacKenzie had appointed her as her personal secretary for all official Halloween dance committee correspondence.

At first Jessica just stared at us really mean.

Then she snatched the letter right out of my hand.

"It's about time you wrote MacKenzie an apology letter. The poor girl was traumatised. Now let's just hope she accepts it. If I was her, I sure wouldn't!"

I couldn't believe Jessica actually said that.

When MacKenzie opens our letter, she'll be in for a little surprise. And, of course, she'll probably have a big hissy fit and create a lot of drama.

I'm going to need years of intensive therapy just to recover from having a locker next to that girl.

BTW, today in biology, Brandon barely said hi and then ignored me the entire hour.

I'm guessing that he's mad at me too.

It sometimes feels like the ENTIRE world is mad at me.

WHATEVER!!! ☹!!

Today we started the gymnastics section in gym class.

I think I might actually be allergic to gymnastics, because whenever I get within ten feet of a piece of equipment, I break out in a rash.

Our gym teacher placed Chloe and Zoey in the intermediate group because they were both pretty good.

But I got stuck in the beginner group because she said I needed a lot of work on "fundamental skills".

The first fundamental skill she requested that I master was "not falling off".

Surprisingly, I caught on really fast.

And, with courage and discipline, I had the potential of earning a perfect score of 10. Just like those girls on the Olympic gymnastics team.

ME ON THE BALANCE BEAM, "NOT FALLING OFF".

ME ON THE UNEVEN BARS, "NOT FALLING OFF".

ME ON THE VAULT, "NOT FALLING OFF".

My gym teacher said she was really proud of the progress I had made in class today and gave me a B+.

I now have a renewed respect for gymnasts, especially those who have completely mastered "not falling off".

Since MacKenzie is in our gym class, I was not that

surprised when she came over and told Chloe, Zoey and me that she was having another emergency meeting today.

She said it was to approve the resignations of some committee members and that attendance was mandatory.

We were happy and relieved she had agreed to let us quit. So we skipped lunch again and went to the auditorium.

MacKenzie opened the meeting by saying that all resignations had to be approved by her. And that until that happened, Chloe, Zoey and I were still official members of the clean-up crew.

Then things started to get really WEIRD.

She became very emotional and said, "Due to a recent incident in my life — caused by a person who shall remain nameless — I can no longer serve as chairperson of the dance and I tender my resignation. However, I'll continue to support

404

the dance by attending, _IF_ it actually occurs."

Then, as if on cue, ALL the set-up committee members resigned. Then the food committee members. Then the entertainment, publicity and decoration committees.

MacKenzie smiled really big and said, "As chairperson, I officially approve all the resignations, including my own. All ex-committee members are now free to leave."

The other clean-up crew members and I just sat there in shock as every last person got up and walked out.

Except MacKenzie.

"OMG! It looks like I totally forgot to vote on your resignations. Which, BTW, means YOU five are now the Halloween dance committee. If you decide to have it, you better get busy because you have a ton of work to do. And if you decide to cancel it, make sure you notify Principal Winston and the student council. Although, I wouldn't want to be the one to disappoint the entire school like that. Good luck! LOSERS!"

I just sighed and rolled my eyes at her.

"MacKenzie, you are SUCH a drama queen. You can't just resign like this and walk out!"

"Oh yeah?! WATCH ME!!"

Then she cackled like a witch and sashayed out of the auditorium.

I just HATE it when MacKenzie sashays!

By sixth hour, the entire school was gossiping about how MacKenzie and the other committee members had resigned.

Everyone was saying the Halloween dance was going to be either cancelled or a complete DISASTER!

WHY?

Because no one believed that the clean-up crew —
Chloe, Zoey, me, Violet and Theodore, the biggest
DORKS in the entire school — could pull off the
biggest social event of the semester.

And they were absolutely right.

☹!!

I spent the entire night tossing and turning and barely got any sleep.

I also had the most horrible nightmare.

I was at the Halloween party dancing in a chocolate bar costume.

And for some reason, I couldn't feel my toes, feet or legs.

Suddenly, I realised in horror that my body was melting into a pool of warm, gooey chocolate.

And even though I was desperately screaming for help, everyone at the dance just laughed and started dipping pieces of fruit into my melted body parts.

Talk about TRAUMATISING!

Boy, was I ever relieved when I realised it was all just a silly nightmare.

This morning the members of the clean-up crew had an emergency meeting in the library about the Halloween dance.

Only, it really WAS an emergency because we had to decide whether or not to cancel it.

409

I was in the library writing in my diary and waiting for the others to arrive when Brandon walked in.

I was surprised to see him. Especially since it seemed like he'd been avoiding me the past few days.

Brandon placed a stack of books on the front desk and kind of hesitated like he was a little nervous or something. Then, finally, he walked up to me.

"So, um. . . how's the Halloween dance coming?"

"It's NOT. Haven't you heard? MacKenzie quit. And took practically ALL the committee members with her."

"There's still you and a few others, right?"

"Unfortunately, we'll be having a meeting in the next ten minutes to officially cancel it," I said, glancing at the clock. "I'm just waiting for everyone to arrive."

Brandon folded his arms and sighed. "That's too bad. I was looking forward to going."

I had to admit, he DID look a little disappointed. And for some reason, that bothered me.

"Well, I'm sure you and MacKenzie can find something else to do Halloween night. Maybe you guys can go trick-or-treating?"

I threw my head back and did a fake little laugh to try to hide my snarkiness.

411

"MacKenzie? Who said I was taking MacKenzie?"

"Um. . . everybody!"

"Oh. Well, I guess everybody's wrong, then," Brandon said with a shrug.

I stared at him in disbelief. OMG! Did he just say he WASN'T going with MacKenzie! WHAT?! How could he NOT be going with MacKenzie?

"Well, *somebody* needs to tell her that. She already has your costumes picked out."

Brandon glanced out the library window like our conversation was boring him out of his skull. "I did. She asked me to take her and I said no."

"You told MacKenzie NO?!" I said, trying not to act surprised.

HOW could he say no to MacKenzie? WHY would he say no to MacKenzie? No one EVER says no to MacKenzie!

412

"She said she'd just cancel the whole thing," Brandon said looking really annoyed.

"Okay, wait a minute! Are you serious? MacKenzie said she'd cancel the dance for the entire school unless you agreed to be her date?"

"Something like that."

"How could she?! That's just totally. . . CRAZY!"

"Yeah, she set you guys up."

I tried to wrap my head around everything I'd just heard.

"Okay. So, MacKenzie resigns, and when the dance gets cancelled, nobody ever finds out she lied about you taking her. And in the end the entire school gets mad at US and not HER! UNBELIEVABLE!"

"If you cancel the dance, she wins," Brandon said matter-of-factly.

413

"WOW! This is just so. . . WOW!! I don't know how we'd ever pull it off."

Brandon grinned and winked at me. "You'll figure it out. I'm afraid MacKenzie's met her match."

"Listen, bud. Have you seen the clean-up crew?! Actually, YOU should be afraid! Be VERY afraid!!"

We both laughed really hard at my silly little joke. It was kind of strange, but talking to Brandon not only gave me a whole new perspective on things, it also made me feel A LOT better.

Soon we were talking about school and stuff. That went really well until he smiled at me kind of shylike and stared right into my eyes.

Of course I started blushing like crazy.

Then it got so quiet we could hear the library clock ticking.

I think he felt a little embarrassed too, because he

414

bit his lip and started drumming his fingers on the magazine shelf.

Suddenly he slapped his forehead and gave me this really goofy but cute look.

"Duh! I almost forgot what I came in here for."

"Yeah, me too." I trudged over to the front desk and grabbed his pile of library books to process them back into the system. "It looks like none of these are overdue. So, are you returning—"

Brandon didn't give me a chance to finish. "No, actually, I came in here to ask if you'd go to the dance with me?"

My mouth dropped open and I just stared at him.

I could NOT believe my ears.

"Wait. Did I hear you correctly? You just asked me if—"

"Yeah, I did."

"Oh! Well. . . okay. SURE! I guess," I stammered, blushing more than ever. "IF there is a dance."

I was trying to act nonchalant about the whole thing. But inside my head I was like,

YEESSS ☺!!

"Cool," Brandon said, nodding his head and looking a little relieved. "Very cool. And let me know if I can help you guys out."

"Sure! And thanks! You know. . . for asking me." I was smiling from ear to ear and couldn't stop.

"Hey, no prob. Well, I better get going. See you in bio."

Still a bit dazed, I watched him walk to the door and disappear into the hall.

FINALLY!

Brandon had asked me to the Halloween dance!!!

I was so happy I started doing my Snoopy "happy dance".

La, La, La!
I'M . . .

La, La, La!
SO . . .

La, La, La!
HAPPY!!

Soon Chloe, Zoey, Violet and Theo arrived, and we began our meeting.

When I told them about MacKenzie and why she had bailed on the school dance, they could hardly believe it.

Who would have thunk that girl could be so selfish, devious and manipulative.

Talk about EVIL! MacKenzie makes the Wicked Witch of the West look like Dora the Explorer.

I'm just saying. . . !

By the end of the meeting we had all agreed upon two things.

First, we were NOT going to let MacKenzie get away with her dirty little scheme.

And second, the students of WCD were going to have the best Halloween dance EVER!

Courtesy of the clean-up crew ☺!!

The only thing that bothered me was that I was going to be a little busier than I had anticipated.

I was supposed to be:

1. Helping out at the ballet class Halloween party

2. Working on the dance committee

3. Doing that "My date's a band member!" thingy with Chloe and Zoey

AND

4. Hanging out with Brandon as his official date to the dance!

ALL AT THE SAME TIME!

I've gone from "socially challenged" to "socially chic" in just one day.

But I was pretty sure all the scheduling conflicts would simply work themselves out in the end.

I mean, look at those Hollywood party girls.

Aren't they at every party in every city at the same time all while hanging out with their BFFs and boyfriends?

If they can do it, how HARD can it be?!

And everyone knows those celebutants have a combined IQ lower than an ortho retainer.

The good news is that my days of being a not-so-popular party girl are finally over.

☺!!

Mrs Peach has agreed to let us meet in the library every morning to plan the Halloween dance.

She is such a SWEETHEART!

We had a vote and I got elected chairperson.

Which also means it will be entirely MY fault if the whole thing flops!

Violet is in charge of entertainment. Zoey is in charge of set-up. Chloe is in charge of decorations. Theo is in charge of clean-up.

Everyone wanted me to do publicity so I could make us some really cool posters.

However, we still needed someone to be in charge of food.

And about twenty-four more people to help.

That's when I came up with the brilliant idea to place a new sign-up sheet on the bulletin board right outside the office to try to recruit more volunteers.

Some of the jocks and CCPs are so IMMATURE!

The good news is that we got one new volunteer,
Jenny Chen.

I suggested that everyone ask a friend or two to
help out since we are superdesperate for people.

Brandon stopped by again to take our official
Halloween dance committee picture for the yearbook.

So I guess that means we're official ☺!

After our meeting was over, I planned to surprise

Chloe and Zoey with the exciting news that Brandon asked me to the dance.

I had been dying to tell them since yesterday, but I was waiting for the perfect moment.

I was all set to break the news when we saw their crushes, Jason and Ryan, in the library flirting with two CCP girls.

If Chloe and Zoey had been wondering if those two guys were going to ask them to the dance, they definitely got an answer.

A big fat NO!!

I couldn't believe that Jason and Ryan asked two cheerleaders, Sasha and Taylor, to the dance right in front of Chloe and Zoey like that.

Well, maybe not exactly in front of them since the three of us were kind of spying on them through the bookshelves. But still. . . !!

It was suddenly VERY obvious to me that the two hours Jason and Ryan had spent dancing with Chloe and Zoey at MacKenzie's party meant nothing at all. Those guys had tossed them away like two used pieces of Kleenex and asked CCP girls to the dance.

Chloe and Zoey were heartbroken.

But they said having a supportive BFF like me made it a lot easier to deal with the emotional wretchedness of their failed romances.

After that there was no way I could bring myself to tell them about Brandon and me going to the dance together.

I felt SO sorry for them.

But I've also got my own problems to worry about. I've been so OBSESSED with the Halloween dance that I TOTALLY forgot we were having a geometry test today.

The teacher gave us a complicated problem, and we had exactly forty-five minutes to find X, Y and Z.

At first I just stared at the page and started to panic.

Then I realised I was making the problem way more complicated than it really was.

I must have turned into a math genius or something because suddenly it was like I totally understood what I was supposed to do.

I ended up completing the test in no time at all.

Then I took a short nap while the other slowpokes tried to finish before the time was up.

When everyone was finally done, the teacher collected our tests, graded them and handed them back to us.

I took one look at mine and was absolutely

CONBAFFLELATED!!

Which, BTW, means confused, baffled and frustrated.

That's when I totally lost it and yelled at my teacher, "Excuse me, but what's with all the red ink? It looks like you had a really bad nosebleed and used my geometry test as a tissue or something!"

But I just said that inside my head, so nobody else heard it but me.

Although, I have to admit, my geometry teacher WASN'T the first person to criticise my maths skills.

Last year I signed up to be a maths tutor for the sixth graders.

I was really happy because it paid a whopping $10 per hour.

And if I put in 100,000 hours of tutoring by the end of the school year, I could make enough money to actually become a millionaire!

With that kind of cash, I could buy vital personal necessities like an iPhone, a designer wardrobe, extra art supplies AND a private helicopter to fly me to and from school every day.

I mean, like, how COOL would it be if I actually owned a helicopter?!

Chloe, Zoey and I would have the best carpool in the entire school.

ME picking up Chloe and Zoey for school

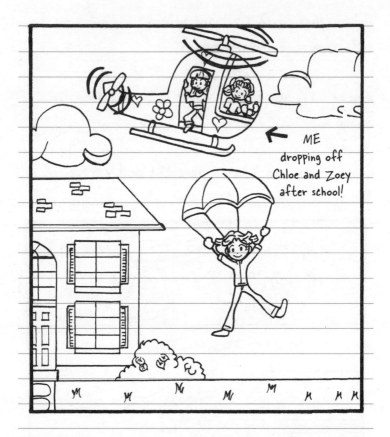

ME dropping off Chloe and Zoey after school!

And MacKenzie and the rest of the CCPs would be SUPERjealous of us.

Anyway, my first week as a maths tutor went really well. I was going to LOVE my exciting new life as a self-made millionaire.

ME,
making a
TON of
MONEY!!

Unfortunately, when everyone got their maths homework back, the complaints started to pour in.

I felt REALLY horrible about the whole thing.

So I tried to say something really positive that would help rebuild their shattered self-esteem.

But I don't think my positive outlook on the situation made anyone feel any better.

So I resigned from my tutoring position and refunded all the money I had been paid.

Mainly because it was the right thing to do.

Plus, I'm VERY allergic to angry mobs.

OMG!! I had such a severe reaction, I thought I was going to have to call an ambulance or something.

Thank goodness my geometry teacher drops our lowest test score before she calculates our final maths grade for the term.

But still! If my parents find out I just failed my geometry test, they're going to

KILL ME!!☹!!

ARRRGGGGGHHH!!

I'm so FURIOUS with MacKenzie Hollister, I could. . .
literally just. . . SPIT!

Not only did she totally RUIN the chances of the
school having a dance by quitting at the last minute,
but she made sure everything was left in total
CHAOS.

I had no idea the situation was so bad until I asked each committee member to present a status report at our meeting this morning.

Zoey went first. She said MacKenzie had arranged for the parents of some of the CCPs to cover the expense of having the dance at the same country club as her birthday party.

However, when Zoey called to find out the set-up time, she was told that our reservation for the dance had been CANCELLED by the previous chairperson.

Since the CCPs were no longer involved with the dance, their parents were no longer paying for it to be held at the country club.

Which meant we didn't have a location for the dance ☹!

That's when I suggested that Zoey ask Principal Winston about using the gym or the cafeteria.

But Zoey said she had already checked.

The cafeteria wasn't available because the Junior League was having a UNICEF fund-raiser and the gym wasn't available because the floor was scheduled to be refinished for basketball season.

"Basically, we don't have a place for the dance. And we don't have any money to PAY for a place for the dance. That's the end of my report. Any questions?" Zoey said, and collapsed into her seat.

Nobody had any questions. Which, BTW, was a good thing, because Zoey was NOT in a very good mood right then.

I thanked Zoey for sharing her very thorough and informative report.

Violet's report for the entertainment committee was next.

She said the band for the dance had also been cancelled by the previous chairperson. The band was

436

no longer available, but their manager was giving us a full refund. In ten days.

"So far I haven't found any bands that are available next week or willing to work for FREE. Which means we don't have any music for the dance."

I thanked Violet for sharing her very thorough and informative report.

It was the same story with decorations and food.

Chloe said that the order for Halloween decorations had been cancelled, and Jenny said the caterer had been cancelled. And both Chloe and Jenny were expecting refunds. AFTER the dance.

Theo added that IF there was a dance, he was definitely willing to clean up after it.

I had my entire reputation on the line as chairperson of the Halloween dance. But, thanks to MacKenzie, we had no location, no band, no decorations and no food.

And to ensure that the dance was a total FLOP, she had arranged it so we wouldn't have a single dime to PAY for a location, a band, decorations or food.

We took a vote and it was a unanimous decision. The Halloween dance was officially

CANCELLED!

It got really sad and quiet in the room and I felt like crying.

And even though all of this WASN'T our fault, I couldn't help but feel like we had let down the entire school.

The worst part was that I was the one stuck with announcing the bad news to the student body.

Which I decided to put off until Monday.

Very soon the black slime mold in the locker room shower was going to be more popular than me.

After school my dad told me to take care of the leaves in the backyard. I was supposed to rake and Brianna was supposed to put them in plastic bags.

I HATE, HATE, HATE

having to do chores with Brianna 🙁!!

439

It took me HOURS to get those leaves into a big pile and Brianna was no help WHATSOEVER!

Thanks to Brianna, I ended up with leaves, twigs and other crud stuck in my hair. I actually looked like I had a new afro hairstyle or something!

I was so MAD! I wanted to stuff her inside a plastic bag and set her out on the curb to be hauled away with the leaves.

But, of course, you can't do that kind of stuff to your little sister or brother, even when they really deserve it. Plus, it probably won't go over that well with your parents.

WHY, WHY, WHY was I not born an ONLY child???!!!

☹!!

I have a terrible headache and I've been feeling superdepressed all day ☹.

I've pretty much given up on the Halloween dance.

Short of a major miracle, it's NOT going to happen.

Plus, I have more important things to worry about.

Like, for example, my nutty sister, Brianna. Her fairy phobia seems to be growing worse.

I think Mom and Dad should seriously consider getting her into some type of counselling or therapy.

Every single night for the past week Brianna has woken me up to go to the bathroom with her because she's afraid.

The fact that she was waking me up in the middle of the night WASN'T the thing that was really bothering me.

It was HOW she was waking me up that was driving me NUTZ!

I considered myself very lucky that Brianna hadn't POKED my eye out yet.

So I did what any perfectly normal, sleep-deprived, raving MANIAC would do in my situation.

I promised Brianna I'd KILL — I mean, get rid of — the tooth fairy so she could start going to the bathroom by herself. Then I could start sleeping nights again.

So in the wee hours of the morning, Brianna and I snuck downstairs to the kitchen so we could make up a special spray that would keep the tooth fairy away.

NIKKI'S HOMEMADE FAIRY REPELLENT

1 cup bottled spring water

3/4 cup vinegar

1/2 cup strained tuna fish oil

1/2 cup strained sardine oil

1 teaspoon ground garlic

1 teaspoon onion powder

Pour ingredients into bottle and shake vigorously for 1 minute or until mixed. For best results, spray liberally in areas where fairy is not wanted. Will repel fairies and most flying insects for 23 years. Excess can be refrigerated and stored for up to 7 days for use as a zesty vinaigrette salad dressing.

Okay, I admit I just made up the recipe right there on the spot to trick Brianna into believing the fairy repellent would actually work.

I poured the liquid into an empty spray bottle and it actually looked pretty real. The only small problem was that the spray SMELLED a lot like a dead walrus. On a hot summer day. In Phoenix, Arizona.

Fairy Repellent

Brianna was nervous about the whole thing and was afraid the fairy might get mad at us if I sprayed her.

Kind of like that time Dad sprayed those hornet wasps and they chased him around the garden for five minutes until he hid behind some rubbish cans.

It was my brilliant idea for me to wear protective gear. I didn't have a choice but to play along to get Brianna to believe the fairy spray would actually work.

After rummaging through her toy box, Brianna handed me her blue plastic diving mask with a snorkel attached.

She said it would help keep the spray out of my eyes and prevent the fairy from gouging them out if she got, like, REALLY violent.

Although, to be honest, I was more worried about Brianna gouging out my eyes than some fairy.

Then Brianna gave me her toy tennis racket with a broken string to use as a fairy swatter.

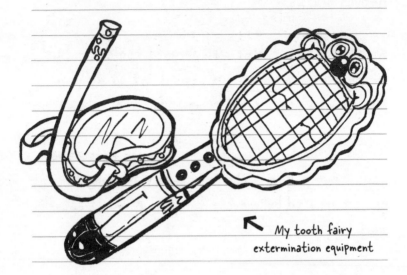

← My tooth fairy extermination equipment

Unfortunately, as soon as I put on the face mask, it started to fog up.

And I was having a hard time breathing through that snorkel.

I felt like the

SPRAY-ER-NATOR!

HASTA LA VISTA, FAIRY!

I sprayed Brianna's bed, desk, lamp and chair with the fairy repellent.

Then I sprayed behind her curtains and inside her toy box.

I was just about to call it a night when Brianna started pulling stuff out from under her bed so I could spray under there.

Then she began tossing junk out of her closet so I could spray in there too.

And she insisted that I spray her Hello Kitty backpack, Barbie CD player and Tickle Me Elmo doll, just to be safe.

I tried to convince Brianna that she had absolutely nothing to worry about.

Because IF the tooth fairy WAS in fact hanging around her room, she was probably totally dripping in stink by now. That poor fairy was going to have to rush back to fairyland and soak in a tub of Mr Bubbles, tomato juice and disinfectant for at least a week.

But Brianna started whining really loud and saying we needed to spray her sock and underwear drawer.

I was like, "Shhhh! You better quiet down before you wake up Mom and Dad! Or we'll BOTH be in big trouble!!"

Soon the spray bottle started making gurgling sounds because it was empty.

I was trying to get out the last few drops when
suddenly the doorknob clicked and the bedroom door
slooooowly opened.

Brianna and I both stared at the door and then each other.

I was like, What the. . . ??!!

"Oh, no! It's the F-F-FAIRY!" Brianna stuttered in horror.

Then she dived into her closet and slammed the door behind her.

Unfortunately, it wasn't the fairy.

I almost wish it had been.

Instead, it was . . .

MOM and DAD!!☹

And I could tell that they were NOT happy.

But what really weirded me out was that my dad's right eye started twitching.

I guessed that it was probably because the room reeked of sardines, tuna fish and vinegar.

Okay. I could understand why my parents might have been a little upset.

It was 2:00 a.m. and we had just totally trashed Brianna's room.

And sprayed enough repellent to fumigate two small, very smelly, fly-infested pig farms.

That's when it occurred to me that, just maybe, I had taken the whole fairy prank thing a bit too far.

To make matters worse, I think the spray was starting to make me feel light-headed and dizzy.

Or maybe I was suffering from oxygen deprivation due to breathing through that snorkel for fifteen continuous minutes.

I thought about hiding the bottle of fairy repellent

and the toy tennis racket behind my back and trying to act natural.

As natural as I could considering the fact that I was in my pyjamas wearing a blue plastic diving mask with a snorkel.

My parents were still just standing there with shocked looks on their faces.

Unfortunately, that snorkel thingy made my voice and breathing sound just like Darth Vader's.

But with a really wicked lisp.

"Hi, Dag! Hi, Mog! *Cheee-whoooo.* Whath up! I'm willy berry thorry I woke you up. *Cheee-whoooo.* I wuz justh working on my scieneth project and Brianna's room got a bit methy. *Cheee-whoooo.* LUKE, I AM YOUR FATHER!! *Cheee-whoooo.*"

Lucky for me, Mom and Dad laughed at my joke.

Then I explained that I was just testing out a

new homemade insect repellent/vinaigrette salad dressing/air freshener called Sardine Summer Splash.

And that it was an extra-credit homework assignment.

For gym class.

And extra credit is a good thing!

When Brianna came crawling out of the closet, I knew I was dead meat. I was going be grounded forever if she spilled about my little prank.

But she totally backed me up and told Mom and Dad she had helped me make a special spray to get rid of a little pest in her bedroom.

Thank goodness she didn't tell them the pest was the tooth fairy!

My parents just assumed it was a bug or something and believed the whole story.

457

I just hope Brianna has finally got over her fairy phobia.

One thing is for sure. . .

It'll be really nice to start sleeping again without having to worry about waking up to find one of my eyeballs lying on my pillow looking at me.

EWWW!

HOW GROSS WOULD *THAT* BE!!

It's the wee hours of the morning and I'm so exhausted I can hardly keep my eyes open.

Mrs Hargrove stopped by this evening to drop off the face-painting supplies for the ballet class Halloween party next Thursday.

She also gave me a rubbish bag that contained a "supercute costume".

She said her niece bought it especially for me to wear to the party and they just knew the kids were going to love it.

That's when I started to get this really bad feeling about Mrs Hargrove's niece.

I was like, "Oh, by the way, I don't think you ever told me your niece's name. Since she goes to WCD, I probably know her."

"Actually, she's one of your good friends. MacKenzie

Hollister! She said you guys have lockers right next to each other and you came to her birthday party last week."

"MacKenzie?!" I gulped.

For a split second it felt like I was going to lose the meat loaf I had eaten for dinner.

"Um. . . yeah. I guess you could say MacKenzie and I are really good . . . locker neighbours."

I vaguely remembered overhearing MacKenzie mention an aunt Clarissa back in September.

My head was spinning as I thanked Mrs Hargrove and trudged upstairs to my room.

WHY in the world had MacKenzie told her aunt I was the best artist in the school?!

Especially after she had compared my artwork to poodle vomit.

And WHY had she suggested that I paint faces for the ballet class Halloween party?!

One thing was VERY clear to me. I smelled a RAT! A really big, stinky RAT!!

LITERALLY.

Inside the bag was the most hideous-looking rat costume I had ever seen in my life.

And it totally reeked of sweaty armpits, stale pizza and disinfectant spray.

I almost gagged.

I guessed that the costume was probably the mascot for some popular restaurant for kids. But it smelled so bad that customers had complained and the manager had thrown it away.

Then, after it had been buried in a Dumpster full

of rubbish for weeks, some high school kid found it and sold it on eBay for $3 to fund his iTunes addiction.

MacKenzie bought it and then gave it to her aunt to give to ME!

Sometimes I wonder if I'm the only person at my school who believes Satan's kid sister has a locker right next to mine.

Anyway, I started feeling really sorry for myself.

While most students in our city would be attending their school's Halloween dance, I was going to be stuck at the Westchester Petting Zoo wearing a stank rat costume and entertaining a bunch of bratty little ballerinas.

How DEPRESSING! I felt like crying just thinking about it.

While everyone else was having fun, I'd be having a BOO-HOO at the ZOO!! ☹!!

463

My life was so PATHETIC it made me want to—

Suddenly the craziest idea popped into my head!

I tried really hard to ignore it, hoping it would just crawl back into the deep recesses of my brain or wherever crazy ideas come from.

Then I thought, Why not? What do I have to lose?

I rushed over to my computer, went online and did a search for local Halloween haunted houses.

Lucky for me, the place I was interested in was open on Sundays until 7:00 p.m.

I called and spoke with the manager of the facility and explained my situation. He was in complete agreement with my plan as long as we secured permission from Principal Winston.

Since the future of our dance was in limbo, I placed the guy on hold and called Principal Winston's home number, hoping that the three

464

of us could speak together in a conference call.

I started by apologising profusely for disturbing Principal Winston at his home on a Sunday evening and explained that I had an urgent matter to discuss.

However, it took me a while to convince him that I wasn't a prank caller and that the manager of a haunted house really needed to speak with him ASAP regarding a school function.

Within ten minutes all the details had been hammered out and Principal Winston gave me permission to move forward with my plan.

I was ecstatic and started doing my Snoopy "happy dance". AGAIN!!

La, La, La!
I'M . . .

La, La, La!
SO . . .

La, La, La!
HAPPY!!

Next I e-mailed everyone on the dance committee:

HI EVERYONE,
MEET ME IN THE LIBRARY ON
MONDAY AT 7:00 A.M.
FOR AN EMERGENCY MEETING!!
AND BE READY TO ROCK ☺!!
NIKKI

Then I ran downstairs and raided the refrigerator.

I'm pulling an all-nighter and need every ounce of energy I can get my hands on to stay awake.

WHY?

Because the WCD Halloween dance is back on with a vengeance!

Due to the pure GENIUS of one very FIERCE chairperson.

Namely. . . ME! ☺

466

My new idea for our Halloween dance is totally

KA-RAY-ZEE!

But in a really good way.

OMG! It's almost 6:00 a.m. and our meeting is in one hour.

Gotta go shower and eat breakfast. . . !

I didn't get any sleep last night, so I'm superexhausted. But I'm also deliriously HAPPY ☺!!

BOO!!
(AT THE ZOO)

WCD Middle School
Annual Halloween Dance

Thursday, October 31st
7:30 p.m. to 11:00 p.m.

A Most Frightening Experience at the

WESTCHESTER ZOO
HALLOWEEN HAUNTED HOUSE

We've plastered the ENTIRE school with our posters and flyers!

469

And now everyone is buzzing about the dance. Which, BTW, is being held on the premises of the biggest haunted house in the city, sponsored annually by the Westchester Zoo.

I've heard "Boo at the ZOO" a million times already and it's not even third hour yet.

There are so many students wanting to help out that I had to put up another volunteer sign-up sheet and then add a second page.

Our meeting this morning went really well and turned into a big brainstorming session. And by the time it was over, thirty-nine people had shown up.

Zoey reported that the Westchester Zoo was happy to host our dance at no charge and set-up was going to be from 3:00 to 6:00 p.m. on Thursday, October 31.

Chloe reported that the art classes were making an assortment of Halloween decorations for extra credit. And the maths club was donating two dozen pumpkins they planned to carve using equilateral, isosceles and scalene triangles.

Violet reported that she still hadn't found a band that would play for free. But since she had an iTunes collection of 7,427 songs, she could throw together a playlist and be our resident DJ.

Theo added that he and a few members of the jazz band had started a group and were willing to do a forty-five-minute set for free, just for the experience of performing before a live audience.

Jenny said that the home-ec classes had agreed to bake chocolate chip cookies and cupcakes. And she had arranged for the owners of Pizza Palace to donate punch, pizzas and assorted flavours of wing-dings with dipping sauces.

Then the science club members volunteered to help with both set-up and clean-up.

I could NOT believe everything for the dance had fallen right into place like that!

Although, I still hadn't made up my mind about my Halloween costume.

ZOEY

Chloe and Zoey had made it very clear that they hated my bag of trash idea. So I decided to wear Mom's Juliet costume.

Zoey says she is going to be Beyoncé, since she looks a lot like her. She's going to wear an outfit from Beyoncé's latest video and sign autographs at the dance.

CHLOE

Chloe says she wants to be the character Sasha Silver from her favourite book series, *Canterwood Crest*. It's about these frenemies at a private riding academy and it's kind of like

The Clique, but on horseback. Chloe plans to wear fancy riding gear with boots.

And Brandon says he's going to be one of the Three Musketeers. How COOL is THAT?! I can't wait to see him.

Now that I think about it, I'm really glad we're not doing my bag of rubbish costume idea.

I'd be totally embarrassed to have Brandon see me wearing something so immature and silly.

BTW, I still haven't told Chloe and Zoey yet that Brandon asked me to go to the dance.

I was going to tell them last week, but when the dance got cancelled, I figured, why bother?

Although, to be honest, I'd rather just keep it a secret for now.

I guess I'm really worried Brandon is going to change his mind for some reason.

473

And then I'll be so HUMILIATED I'll have to transfer to a new school or something.

But I know I have to tell Chloe and Zoey sooner or later.

Definitely. . . LATER!

Now that the Halloween dance is back on again, I don't think I'm going to have time to go trick-or-treating with Brianna this year.

I'm kind of bummed out because I've done Halloween ever since I was a little kid and it's always been such a blast!

Except for that one year when Chucky Reynolds, the neighbourhood bully, started snatching kids' trick-or-treat bags.

He stole MY sweets too! However, instead of getting mad, I decided to get even. And I waited until the next Halloween to do it.

Our neighbour had a vegetable garden and I noticed there were like a zillion worms in her compost pile. So I knocked on her door and asked her really politely if I could borrow two cups of worms. She looked at me like I was crazy, but she said yes.

Needless to say, I ran into Chucky on Halloween night. And when he demanded that I hand over my treats, I was actually kind of happy about it.

Chucky the Bully

ME

My little trick worked perfectly and Chucky
Reynolds NEVER snatched another kid's sweets
again! ☺!!

AAAAAHHHHH!!

Okay. THAT was me screaming!

WHY?

Because I can't believe the HORRIBLE MESS I've got myself into!

AAAAAHHHHH!!

That was me screaming AGAIN!

My situation is BAD! VERY BAD!!

Right before lunch I got a note from
Chloe and Zoey to meet them in the janitor's
closet.

They said they couldn't wait to show me their new
Halloween costumes.

But more than anything, I thought this would be
the PERFECT time to FINALLY tell them about
Brandon asking me to the dance.

Since he hadn't cancelled on me (yet, anyway!) and
the dance was in only two days, I thought now would
be a good time to tell my BFFs.

So this was the plan I had inside my head. . .

After I got done raving about Zoey's Beyoncé
costume and Chloe's *Canterwood Crest* riding
costume, I was going to tell them about MY
fabulous Juliet costume. And maybe even invite
them over to see it after school today.

Then I was going to blurt out:

GUESS WHAT?!
BRANDON ASKED
ME TO
THE DANCE!!

Chloe and Zoey were going to be so surprised that they'd start screaming and jumping up and down.

We'd end the little celebration with a group hug.

I was also pretty sure that during the dance, Chloe and Zoey would insist that I secretly meet them somewhere to give them all the juicy details.

Which meant I'd probably have to tell Brandon I

needed to go to the bathroom, like, once every hour. Just to update my BFFs.

THAT was the PERFECT plan I had inside my head.

But unfortunately, things didn't happen the way I had planned.

When I got to the janitor's closet, I told Chloe and Zoey that I had some surprising news for them too.

They said, "Okay! You first!"

And then I said, "No! You first!"

Then they said, "Come on! YOU go first!"

And then I said, "No way! YOU go first!"

So they finally said, "Okay! We'll go first."

Then they made me close my eyes.

"SURPRISE!! Here's OUR costumes!!"

When I opened my eyes, I was expecting to see a Beyoncé outfit and a riding outfit.

But instead, I saw THREE rubbish bag costumes!!

The exact same rubbish bag costume I had suggested two weeks ago that Chloe and Zoey had called really LAME!

"Aren't they CUTE?!" Chloe said, smiling really big and giving me jazz hands.

"Do you NOT love them?!" Zoey giggled.

"We figured that since the three of us were going to be hanging out at the dance together. . ." Chloe started.

"We might as well hang out as three BAGS OF RUBBISH!" Zoey finished.

"OMG! OMG! You—you guys SHOULDN'T have!" I stammered.

Only, I really meant it.

"Well, since you had your heart set on us being bags of rubbish, we didn't want to let you down. Especially after you agreed to do that clean-up crew thing with us. And if it wasn't for you, we wouldn't even be having a dance," Chloe said, tearing up a little.

"Yeah, we were being a little selfish about the whole costume thing. So after school yesterday, we met at Chloe's and worked on them until midnight. It's the least we can do to show you how much we appreciate having a really great BFF like you!" Zoey said, dabbing her eyes.

"Yeah, one who'll stick by us through thick and thin, no matter what!" Chloe added.

Then Chloe and Zoey both grabbed me and we did a group hug.

Then they said, "Okay. Now what did YOU want to tell US?!"

I just stood there looking at Chloe and Zoey and feeling REALLY horrible!

I couldn't believe they were actually giving up their cool costumes.

To dress up like LAME bags of rubbish?!

JUST FOR ME??!!

I didn't deserve great friends like Chloe and Zoey!

But another part of me felt bad because I knew true friendship was supposed to be based on honesty.

Which meant I had no choice but to tell them the truth. . .

That Brandon had asked me to the dance and I had accepted.

That I planned to mostly hang out with him all night. Not them.

That I was going to be a beautiful, romantic and moody Juliet. NOT a bag of rubbish.

So I just blurted it out.

"I'm really sorry, Chloe and Zoey, but I CAN'T wear

that bag of rubbish costume or hang out with you guys at the dance!"

At first they were confused and kind of stunned.

"What do you mean. . . ?" Zoey sputtered.

"I d–d–don't understand. . . !" Chloe stuttered.

Then, as it sank in, their confusion turned into hurt and they both just stared at me.

Okay, I liked Brandon a lot, and I really, really wanted to go to the dance with him.

But there was NO WAY I could do this to my two best friends.

So I smiled really big and gave them jazz hands to lighten the mood.

"Um. . . what I actually meant was. . . I can't wear that costume or hang out with you guys. . . UNLESS we get yellow rubber gloves, crazy wigs and sunglasses!! We gotta have those! Right?"

Chloe and Zoey looked totally relieved and smiled at me.

"OMG! You almost gave us a heart attack!" Chloe chuckled.

"Rubber gloves, wigs and sunglasses, coming right up!" Zoey said. She opened a bag and tossed one of each to me.

"Great! Then I guess we're ready to ROCK!" I said, smiling.

Even though deep inside I was so frustrated I felt more like crying.

"We're going to have SO much fun!!" Zoey squealed.

"I can hardly wait!!" Chloe giggled.

So that's why I'm now in my bedroom screaming.

486

AAAAAHHHHHH!!

Mainly because Thursday evening could turn into a major DISASTER.

I'm supposed to wear a rat costume and hang out with the ballerina brats.

I'm supposed to wear a Juliet costume and hang out with Brandon.

AND I'm supposed to wear a bag of rubbish costume and hang out with Chloe and Zoey!

All at the same time!

How did I ever get myself into this MESS?!

Okay, here's an idea. . .

I'll just call Brandon, Chloe, Zoey and Mrs Hargrove and tell them I'll be home sick Thursday evening with a bad case of BUBONIC PLAGUE.

This morning at breakfast I was

TOTALLY GROSSED OUT!!

I think I've lost my appetite for the rest of the year.

My mom put my dad on a diet last week and he has started doing midnight raids on the refrigerator. It's very obvious because he forgets to put stuff back in the fridge.

Unfortunately, I always know at breakfast when he's had cookies and milk the night before.

Hey, call me a picky eater! But, personally,
I don't like my Fruity Pebbles with sour milk
chunks.

If this keeps up, I think I'll need to have a little talk with Mom about this situation.

I'll remind her that marriage is based on mutual love, trust and respect, and that she didn't marry Dad for his looks.

But, most important of all, I'll gently bring up the fact that Dad gaining a few extra pounds won't really matter when I DIE OF STARVATION because all the food in the house is SPOILED!

I'm just saying. . . !!

Anyway, right now I'm feeling like the most HORRIBLE person on earth ☹!

I can't believe I'm LYING to my friends like this!

Well, if not exactly lying, I'm NOT telling them important stuff they should probably know.

I haven't told Brandon, Chloe or Zoey that I'm

491

supposed to be helping out at the ballet class party during the dance.

I haven't told Chloe and Zoey I'm supposed to be Brandon's date to the dance.

And I haven't told Brandon I'm supposed to be hanging out with Chloe and Zoey all night as bags of rubbish.

WHY?

Because I'm trying really hard to make everyone HAPPY.

The last thing I want is for Brandon, Chloe or Zoey to be disappointed in me as a friend.

But if I tell them the truth, all three of them will probably HATE me!

Unless I secretly try to. . . ??

NO WAY!!

It will NEVER work!!

Besides, I'm NOT a lying, sneaky little RAT, like MacKenzie!

Or am I . . .?!

☹!!

MACKENZIE

ME

THURSDAY, OCTOBER 31

Okay, this is probably the longest diary entry in the entire history of the world.

But that's because tonight was

UNBELIEVABLE!

Thank goodness we don't have school on Friday due to parent-teacher conferences. I'm TOTALLY EXHAUSTED and barely have enough energy to write this!

Brianna's ballet class party started at 7:00 p.m. at the petting zoo.

Lucky for me, it was only one building over from the zoo's haunted house, which was where we were having our Boo at the Zoo dance.

Mom dropped me off fifteen minutes early so I could change into my rat costume.

The eyeholes must have been made for a taller
person, because I was too short to see out of them.

The best I could do was peek through one of the rat's enormous nostrils.

All I had to do was paint some faces and lead a few games and then I was OUTTA THERE!

Most of the girls in the ballet class were wearing cute little animal costumes because of the petting zoo theme.

My sister, Brianna, was the Easter Bunny. Actually, a PSYCHOPATHIC Easter Bunny.

She gathered all the other kids around her and then yelled at the top of her lungs, "Hi, there! I'm the real, live Easter Bunny! Since you all have been good little girls, would you each like a GIGANTIC CHOCOLATE BUNNY?!!"

Of course everyone got really excited and shouted, "YEEESSSSS!"

I could NOT believe what Brianna said next!

It's pretty obvious that my kid sister has some SERIOUS issues!

She didn't have the slightest idea I was Mr Rat and I decided not to tell her.

Hanging out with the girls and painting their faces was actually kind of fun.

A unicorn told me everything she wanted for Christmas, like I was Santa Claus or somebody.

And this cute little witch whispered into my huge rat ear that if I came to her house in the middle of the night and bit off all her brother's toes, she would keep it a secret!

Just in case I wanted to do something like that.

And I felt really bad because I think I may have traumatised this cute little cat.

She pointed at me and shrieked, "I'm scared! That big kangaroo is stinky and has eyes inside his nose!!"

I was like, AMEN, SISTER!!

After I finished painting faces, I led several rounds of the Hokey Pokey dance. It must have been 120 degrees inside that costume.

I was relieved when Mrs Hargrove asked the girls to be seated for pizza and punch.

I decided to sneak away for a while and told

Mrs Hargrove I was going to take a short toilet break.

I grabbed my duffel bag and raced back to the bathroom.

It felt good to finally get out of that smelly rat getup.

I splashed cold water on my face and arms to cool down and freshen up.

But my heart was pounding from the excitement of what I was about to try to pull off.

Within minutes I had completely changed into my Juliet costume.

I pinned on the wig thingy, smoothed on three layers of Very Berry Krazy Kiss lip gloss and then gazed at my reflection in the mirror.

It took a few seconds for me to get over the shock of what I saw.

I barely recognised myself!

I threw my duffel bag over my shoulder and hurried down to the haunted house, which was located in the zoo's community centre.

Once inside, I found the nearest bathroom and hung my bag on the hook behind the door of the very last stall.

I put on my mask, walked back down the hall and stepped inside the dance.

Even though it had just started, the room was already packed with people. The decorations and food we had brought in looked fabulous!

And the whole haunted house scene with the antique furniture, cobwebs, and assorted animated witches, ghosts and ghouls that randomly popped out of coffins and closets really helped set the fun mood.

Even though I was Juliet, I felt more like Cinderella because everyone around me was staring.

Most of the CCP girls just glared and whispered.

The crazy thing was that nobody seemed to recognise me. And I wasn't that worried about Chloe and Zoey because they were up front helping Violet with the music.

Violet was onstage rocking the house with some hot tunes by Justin Bieber! I think she was supposed to be an evil clown or something, but I couldn't really tell.

That girl is TOO weird. But in a good way.

I couldn't wait to see Brandon. When I finally spotted him, I couldn't help but stare.

OMG! He looked SO handsome in his costume. I thought I was going to faint!

I think he was really surprised by my costume too because he blinked a few times and then just stared right back at me.

We just stood there kind of staring at each other for what seemed like forever.

It wasn't until I said, "Hi, Brandon," that he finally seemed sure it was actually me.

He brushed his hair out of his eyes, smiled and offered me a seat.

"Wow! Nikki, you look, I mean, your costume is really. . . cool."

"Thanks, Brandon. I think you make a great Mouseketeer!"

"Um. . . it's 'Musketeer.'"

"Oh, sorry! Musketeer."

"So. . . would you like to dance?"

"Sure!"

Thank goodness it was a fast song.

Brandon was actually a pretty good dancer. And he was cracking jokes the entire time, which made me laugh really hard.

We were having so much fun I didn't want the song to end.

We were just about to sit down again when I saw Chloe and Zoey heading in our direction.

I was like, UH—OH!

"Brandon, I think I'm going to go to the bathroom and then check on a few things, okay?"

"Sure. I'll be waiting right here."

"Would you like me to bring you anything back? Like some. . . wing-dings?"

"Wing-dings. Um, sounds. . . interesting!

"You're gonna love 'em! Back in a few minutes!"

I headed for the door.

And I got there just in time.

When I peeked back inside, I saw Chloe and Zoey talking to Brandon. Then he pointed in my direction.

I took off running like a maniac down the hall to the bathroom.

I slammed the stall door shut and frantically pulled
off the dress and wig and stuffed them into my
duffel bag.

Then I slipped into the rubbish bag costume and tied
the drawstrings into a bow at my neck.

My fingers nervously fumbled as I put on the hot
pink wig, sunglasses and rubber gloves.

Finally.

FINISHED!!

And not a second too soon. Just as I was coming out of the stall, Chloe and Zoey rushed in.

"Hi, Nikki! We've been waiting on you. Brandon told us you were in here. Isn't this great?" Chloe said breathlessly.

"I'm so happy we decided to go with your costume idea! We look SO cute!" Zoey gushed, posing in the mirror.

"Hey, girlfriends! It's time for us to take out the rubbish!" I teased.

We did a quick group hug and rushed into the dance.

Just about everyone was out on the floor having fun. Even the teachers.

I totally avoided the side of the room where Brandon was sitting and prayed he couldn't see me because of the crowd and dim lights.

Although, even if he had, there was no way he would have recognised me. He was not expecting to see me in a wacky rubbish bag costume, and the wig and sunglasses practically covered my entire face.

Chloe, Zoey and I had a blast dancing!

But I was starting to get a little worried about being away from the ballet party for too long.

"Um, guys, I ran into Brandon a few minutes ago and convinced him to try some of our yummy punch and wing-dings. I was going to take him some snacks, but I just found out I have to go drop off papers at the zoo office. Could one of you take Brandon over some punch and a plate of wing-dings and let him know I had to run an errand?"

"Sure!" Chloe said, and headed off towards the food table.

"Hey! I'll come with you," Zoey said, following me out into the hall.

I started to panic.

"NO!! Zoey, you can't!" I almost screamed at her.

She froze and just kind of stared at me, wondering why I was freaking out like that.

I plastered a fake smile on my face and tried to regain my composure.

"Actually, what I meant was, um. . . no, you CAN'T miss this really great party! I'll be back in a sec, 'kay?"

Zoey shrugged and smiled. "Sure!"

As soon as she was out of sight, I sprinted back to the bathroom.

I dived into the last stall, changed back into that funky-smelling rat costume and hightailed it back to the ballet party.

I was superworried because I had taken a heck of a long toilet break.

But it was perfect timing because the girls were just finishing up their dessert of Steaming Witches' Brew Ice Cream Punch and Worms-'n'-Mud chocolate cupcakes.

"Oh, there you are!"

Mrs Hargrove rushed over and tried to peer in at me through the rat's left nostril.

"I think we're ready for another game," she said.

I gave her the thumbs-up sign.

But in my head I was like, WHEW!!

We played Simon Says and Duck, Duck, Goose! and the kids loved it.

Soon Ranger Roger arrived to take the kids around to see the animals.

Since the kids were going to be distracted for the next half hour, I told Mrs Hargrove that the rat costume had got a little warm and I was going to step outside for a few minutes to cool down.

I grabbed my duffel bag, raced to the bathroom and changed back into my Juliet costume.

Within three minutes I was back at the Halloween dance sitting next to Brandon.

"Hey! You're back." His smile could have lit up the entire room.

"Sorry. I just had a few errands to take care of! I'm, like, the most horrible date!"

"No, I don't mind, really. I figured you were going to be kind of busy tonight."

"Thanks for understanding."

Then it got really quiet and I just kind of stared at him with this stupid smile on my face.

I started to get butterflies in my stomach.

That's when I decided to say something witty and intelligent.

"Soooo. . . how did you like those wing-dings?"

"Actually, they were pretty good."

"I just knew you would like them!"

"Oh, I was supposed to let Chloe and Zoey know when you got back. I think I'll just text message them. . ."

"Um, you know what?! Boy, am I hungry! I think I'm going to run over and get us both some more wing-dings. 'Kay? Be right back!"

"Hey, wait! I'll go with—"

But I disappeared before he finished his sentence.

Chloe and Zoey had made their way back to Brandon's table by the time I reached the door.

I raced back to my bathroom stall to change again.

Okay, rubbish bag, rubber gloves, sunglasses and. . . rat head!

NOPE! Wrong party!

Hot pink wig was what I needed.

I tried to calm down.

But knowing that Chloe and Zoey could pop into the bathroom at any second looking for me made me a nervous wreck.

I was back in my rubbish bag costume and at the food table getting more wing-dings when Chloe and Zoey caught up with me again.

"Hi, Nikki! There you are!"

"Brandon said you went to get more wing-dings."

"Yeah! They're delish!!" I said. "So, where do you guys want to sit?"

"Brandon said we could sit with him. There's plenty of room at his table."

"SIT TOGETHER?!" I gasped. "Sure. Umm. . . you two go right ahead. I have to, um. . . go to

516

the. . . bathroom. So I'll meet you guys at the table. 'Kay!"

Suddenly I remembered Brandon's snacks. There was no way I could let him see me in my trash bag costume, so I asked Chloe and Zoey for help.

Umm. . . could you guys give Brandon this little plate of wing-dings for me?

Then I took off running as fast as I could.

ARGH! There was NO WAY I could sit with all three of them.

What was I going to do?!

But my bigger headache was that I had barely two minutes to get back to the ballet party.

I ran to the bathroom stall, changed back into the rat costume and rushed over to the petting zoo.

Ranger Roger was finishing up just as I arrived.

Mrs Hargrove handed me a box of goody bags and peered at me through the rat's right nostril. "As soon as you give these out to the girls, you'll be done," she said, smiling.

I was like, YES!!

I could not believe my crazy scheme was actually working.

Since the ballet party was almost over, parents were lining up at the front door to pick up their kids.

I decided to close out the party in a dramatic way.

"Well goodbye, kiddies! I hope you all had fun with

518

Mr Rat! I'm on my way to Disney World to visit my cousin Mickey! Bye, bye!"

All of the kids waved goodbye, and a few of them even looked a little sad to see me go.

Just a few minutes more and the whole funky rat fiasco would be history.

I was heading towards the back door when Brianna yelled, "Hey, wait, Mr Rat! Can I come with you?"

"Yeah! I wanna come too!" said the little girl who had tried to convince me to come to her house and chew off her brother's toes.

Pretty soon the whole group of kids was crowding around and begging to come with me.

"I'm really sorry. Maybe next time, okay?"

I turned around to leave but suddenly realised there was a slight complication—

—Courtesy of my bratty sister, Brianna. I couldn't believe this was actually happening to me!

"I'm not gonna let go of your tail until you promise to take us with you!" Brianna screamed.

I had to think fast!

The rat costume was starting to give me an itchy rash and Brianna would not let go of my tail.

I was sure Chloe, Zoey and Brandon were wondering what had happened to me.

"Okay, I have an idea! Everyone close your eyes and make a wish. Then count to ten. And when you open your eyes, you'll all have a wonderful wish to take home with you! Okay!"

All the girls jumped up and down and cheered together. "YEAHHH!!"

"Hey, Mr Rat! I'm gonna wish that I can go to Disney World with you to visit your cousin Mickey!" Brianna said stubbornly.

I was like, Sheeeeesh! Brianna, just let it go, will you?!

"Now let's all close our eyes and start counting. One, two. . ."

All the girls closed their eyes and counted with me.

"Three, four. . ."

I grabbed my duffel bag and flung it over my shoulder.

"Five, six. . ."

I opened the back door. . .

"Seven, eight. . ." And ran for my life!

And I didn't stop running until I had made it safely back to the dance.

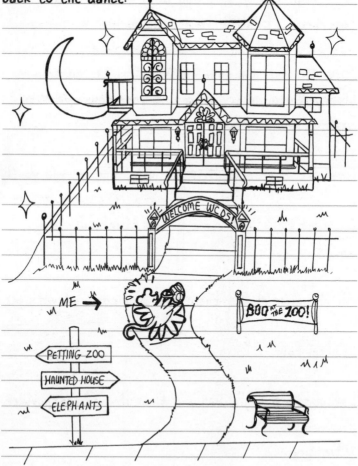

I felt really guilty having to ditch the ballet class like that, but I didn't have a choice.

Although I meant well, all the deception and running back and forth was exhausting.

The dance was going to be over in less than two hours and I planned to enjoy every minute of it.

That's when I decided to ditch the costumes and just have fun hanging out with Zoey, Chloe, and Brandon as plain ol'. . . ME!

All I had to do was change out of the rat costume and into my favourite jeans and sweater.

But as soon as I entered the girls' bathroom, I realised one major obstacle was standing in my way.

MACKENZIE HOLLISTER!

She was dressed as a very chic vampire and was at the mirror applying an extra-thick layer of Bloody Mary Really Scary Red lip gloss.

I thought I was going to have a heart attack right there on the spot.

But mostly I was shocked and surprised she had the nerve to even show up at the dance after trying to undermine the whole thing.

MacKenzie was capable of doing anything to anybody to get what she wanted.

And I was pretty sure she'd do everything within her power to totally RUIN this night for me.

I desperately needed to change my clothes and this was the only girls' bathroom in the entire building.

So I decided to just play it cool by pretending I had to use the bathroom.

I was praying she wouldn't recognise my costume — or rather, HER costume, seeing as she was the one who bought it.

I had just grabbed the stall door handle when suddenly MacKenzie whipped around and stared at me.

I instinctively froze. Then, pretending I wasn't me, I nodded my head kind of friendlylike and waved at her.

Her pouty lips turned into a scowl as she narrowed her eyes at me.

I broke into a sweat.

"EWWWW! What's that horrible smell?!"

I didn't dare say a word for fear she might recognise my voice.

So I just sniffed under each of my armpits and frantically fanned the air under each like, P-U!

Then I held my arms out to my sides and shrugged my shoulders as if to say, Sorry 'bout that!

She rolled her eyes at me, turned back to the mirror and continued applying her lip gloss.

THANK GOODNESS! I wasn't sure if my little antics had totally annoyed or totally disgusted MacKenzie. But I was really happy they had worked!

I quickly entered the stall, dropped my duffel bag on the floor, slammed the door shut, locked it and collapsed with relief against the wall.

WHEW! That was close.

Although, to be honest, I found it a little puzzling that MacKenzie didn't recognise the raunchy odour or the dirty, matted rat fur.

I took off the rat head and dropped it on the floor. I couldn't wait to slip off the hot, scratchy costume and then take it home and burn it in our fireplace.

My comfortable jeans, sweater and sneakers were going to feel like heaven.

Suddenly I heard quick footsteps approach my stall.

Before I knew what was happening, a manicured hand wearing Ravishing Red Revenge sparkly nail polish reached right under my door and snatched my duffel bag.

I frantically lunged after the strap and pulled with all my might. But somehow I must have stepped on that stupid rat head or something.

I slipped, lost my balance, fell over backwards and hit the back of my head on the bathroom floor.

OOOWWWWWW!!!!! I moaned. The ceiling above me was spinning like a merry-go-round. I closed my eyes.

I pulled myself up and massaged the back of my head. The pain was quickly subsiding and luckily I didn't feel a lump or anything.

I staggered to my feet, fumbled with the door lock and peeked out.

Just as I had feared, the duffel bag containing all my clothing and personal belongings had completely disappeared.

Along with MacKenzie.

I was sure she hadn't got very far. And if I went charging out into the hallway, I might even catch her.

But I was a little worried that tackling a fellow student at a school function might end up on my permanent record and negatively impact me getting admitted into a major university after graduation.

Hey, you can never be too careful. I hear some colleges are really picky about that kind of stuff.

I could NOT believe all of this was actually happening to me. I was so frustrated I wanted to scream, but I didn't.

MacKenzie had just stolen my clothes and I was stuck in a bathroom stall wearing a stinky rat costume at the WCD Halloween dance after my secret crush, Brandon, had FINALLY asked me to go.

I was like, PLEASE, PLEASE, PLEASE let all of this just be another really bad dream. I wanted to wake up in my comfy bed wearing my heart pj's and think, WOW! *THAT* was the craziest nightmare EVER!

Only, I didn't wake up. Which meant all of this was real ☹!

So, like any normal girl in my situation, I had a massive panic attack right there on the spot. My stomach started to churn and my knees felt weak.

I kept thinking, *If only* I had bought a new phone instead of that stupid dress for MacKenzie's party. Then I could call my mom and have her bring me some clothes.

Finally, I closed my eyes and took three very deep, calming breaths because I really needed it.

Then I sat down on the toilet seat to focus all my energy into coming up with a solution to my problem.

The problem being, of course, that I really, really needed to get my bag from MacKenzie.

And I had two choices.

I could go the dance in my underwear. Or I could wear the rat costume.

It was a very difficult decision, indeed.

But I decided to go with the rat costume mainly because it offered one important advantage.

When the entire WCD student body witnessed a foul-smelling, mangy rat. . .

1. CHASE DOWN MACKENZIE. . .

My clothes

2. SNATCH A DUFFEL BAG FROM HER. . .

SNATCH!

3. AND THEN CHOKE HER UNTIL SHE TURNED BLUE IN THE FACE AND PASSED OUT. . .

THEY'D HAVE NO IDEA IT WAS ACTUALLY ME. ☺!!

So I put on the rat head and rushed back into the dance.

As I entered, two seventh graders dressed as Klingons stared at me and gasped.

"P-U! What is THAT smell?!"

"I don't know, dude! But whatever it is it just burned out all my nose hairs."

I just waved at them both kind of friendlylike.

I squeezed through the crowd and found a spot along the front wall. From there I scanned the entire room trying to locate either MacKenzie or my duffel bag.

I should have known exactly where to find her!

She was sitting next to Brandon, twirling her hair and trying to flirt with him. And he was looking superbored and trying his best to ignore her. All the while probably wondering where the HECK I was.

Poor guy!

HALLELUJAH! I spotted my duffel bag in an empty chair right next to MacKenzie!

I slowly crept over to the long row of tables they were sitting at. And when it appeared that no one was looking, I quickly dove underneath.

It was supergross crawling around under there, but I was very, very desperate to get my duffel bag back.

MacKenzie was so distracted with Brandon that nabbing it was actually a piece of cake. I probably could have stolen the dress she was wearing and she wouldn't have noticed.

I was just superHAPPY to have my bag back!

In a matter of minutes I'd be sitting right next to Brandon, gazing into his dreamy eyes and having fun with Chloe and Zoey.

Or maybe NOT!

As I approached the door, there was a huge commotion.

Most of the students at the dance were crowded in a half circle staring at something. I couldn't tell what.

Everyone was laughing and pointing, and before long the music stopped and the house lights came on.

Since I was chairperson of the dance and it was my personal business to know what was going on, I pushed my way through the crowd to take a look.

I immediately wished that I HADN'T.

"Hey, look, everybody! There's Mr Rat! We found him!" Brianna screamed gleefully, and pointed at me!

Within seconds I was mobbed by the entire ballet class and they started hugging me.

I had a heart attack right there on the spot!

I could NOT believe those little brats had followed me to the dance.

Principal Winston and a few chaperones stood nearby looking very worried.

I was sure they were trying to figure out where all the little kids had come from and what they were doing at a middle school dance.

I walked up to Principal Winston and peeked at him through my left nostril.

"Um, Principal Winston, I know you're wondering what's going on here and I can explain every—"

But that was as far as I got because that's when Mrs Hargrove, my mom and dad and the parents of the other little girls came rushing into the dance.

And they were NOT happy.

It got really loud and confusing because the parents were really upset and demanding to know why Principal Winston had allowed their six-year-olds into a middle school party.

And, of course, Principal Winston was upset and demanding to know why the parents had let their six-year-olds crash his middle school party.

Finally, Principal Winston asked Violet to pass him the microphone.

"Okay, everyone, please quiet down. It looks like all the children are safe and accounted for. But can anyone explain how they got here?"

That's when MacKenzie raised her hand.

Principal Winston motioned for her to come forwards and handed her the microphone. But before she said anything, she put on a fresh layer of lip gloss.

OMG! That girl is SO vain!

"Hello, everyone. I know what happened, and I personally feel it is my duty to make sure everyone knows the truth. . ."

Deep down, I was a little relieved that MacKenzie was going to explain everything so I wouldn't have to.

"It's all HER fault! The RAT! Right there!" MacKenzie snarled and pointed at me.

Everyone in the entire room immediately turned and stared at me. Although I felt SUPERembarrassed, at least no one knew who I was.

I never would have thought I'd be happy to be wearing that rat head.

That's when MacKenzie walked over and snatched it right off my head.

"It's NIKKI MAXWELL's fault! And I think she owes us all an explanation for why she endangered the lives of these poor, innocent children and RUINED our Halloween dance!"

I was so HUMILIATED I wanted to DIE! Plus, it felt like I had a really bad case of hat hair.

Then MacKenzie shoved the microphone into my hand, sashayed over to Principal Winston, folded her arms, and glared at me with this little smirk on her face.

I didn't know what to say or where to begin.

It didn't help that Chloe, Zoey and Brandon had somehow made their way to the front of the crowd.

They were standing a few feet away with these confused looks on their faces, whispering to one another.

I stared at the floor and sighed. It was so quiet in the room you could hear a pin drop.

Principal Winston cleared his throat. "Well, Miss Maxwell, we're waiting. . . ?!"

"Um. . . actually, I had agreed to help out at the ballet class Halloween party, BEFORE I was voted chairperson of the WCD party. I was just trying to do them both at the same time. Which, in hindsight, maybe wasn't such a good idea. Anyway, the girls must have followed me over here. I'm really, really sorry for messing things up. . . !"

When I looked around the room, everyone was just staring at me — Principal Winston, kids from school, teachers, parents, the ballet class and even my family.

I felt really HORRIBLE for having ruined everything for ALL these people!!!

I handed the microphone back to Principal Winston and turned and rushed out of the dance.

I didn't know where I was going, but I had to get out of there.

542

Chloe and Zoey caught up with me in the hall.

"Wait, Nikki. What's going on?!" Chloe asked.

"Yeah! What are you doing in that rat getup? And where is your trash bag costume?!" Zoey added.

But before I could answer, Brandon walked up.

"I was wondering where you were. Why did you change out of your Juliet costume?"

Chloe and Zoey looked at Brandon and then they both narrowed their eyes at me.

"Juliet costume?! What Juliet costume? You were wearing a Juliet costume?!" Chloe sputtered.

"But where's your rubbish bag costume?!" Zoey asked, still confused.

I just stared at the floor and didn't say anything.

"Wait a minute!" Chloe said, folding her arms and

543

glaring at me. "You've been running around all night in three different costumes?! Why are you trying to trick us?"

"If you didn't want to hang out with us tonight, you could have just told us," Zoey said, obviously hurt.

Brandon must have felt sorry for me or something because he came to my defence. "This is all my fault. I asked her to the dance. I didn't know she was supposed to be hanging out with you guys."

Shocked, Chloe and Zoey spun around and both shouted at me. "BRANDON ASKED YOU TO THE DANCE?!!!"

I could NOT believe the mess I had made. "Listen, guys," I muttered, "all I can say is that I'm sorry. Really, really sorry!"

I faced Chloe and Zoey. "I didn't have the heart to tell you about Brandon asking me to the dance after what happened with Jason and Ryan. I knew how important this dance was for you. I just

REALLY wanted to be there for you guys. . ."

Then I turned to Brandon. "So, maybe I should have told you I couldn't go to the dance because I was going to be too busy. I planned to help out with the ballet class party AND hang out with Chloe and Zoey. But I figured I could just try to do it ALL. But now I see that wasn't fair to you."

Chloe, Zoey and Brandon just looked at me and didn't say anything.

I didn't blame them for being angry with me. I was angry at myself.

I was the worst friend EVER!

With tears streaming down my face, I turned and ran down the hall and right out the front door.

Once outside the building, the first thing I did was throw the rat head into some bushes.

I really HATED that thing!

I found a park bench about thirty metres away and flopped down on it in utter despair.

I stared up at the full moon. Other than the faint sound of the zoo animals and the rustling of leaves in the trees, it was a quiet night.

It felt good being outside in the cool night air, even though I felt really bad inside.

It seemed no matter how hard I tried to make something work, it always turned out to be a complete disaster.

I was SUCH a loser ☹!

I sniffed and wiped away my tears.

"Mind if I sit down?"

I thought I was alone, so hearing a voice startled me.

I was surprised to see Brandon standing right behind me. He sat down next to me on the bench.

"I just needed to get some fresh air," I said, trying to pretend like I had not been crying. "I'm REALLY sorry for ruining everything. . ."

"What? Nothing was ruined."

"Yeah, right! Just our date. And the dance. And the kids' Halloween party. . ."

"Actually, hanging out with you tonight has been. . . well, 'exciting' is a really good word."

"Sure, about as exciting as getting a cavity filled."

"Come on! We weren't even HAVING a dance until you took over. Right?"

"Yeah, I guess so."

"And those little kids liked you so much they followed you over here."

"Well, if you put it that way. . ."

"Anyway, I mainly came out here to give you a really important message."

Like I needed any more bad news. I had already ruined two parties in one evening.

I got this huge lump in my throat and felt like I was going to cry again.

"Yeah, I was kind of expecting that. From Principal Winston?" I asked sadly.

"Nope."

"My parents? I'm probably grounded until my eighteenth birthday."

"Nope. A friend."

"I still have friends? After all this, I'm sure Chloe and Zoey wouldn't want to be seen with me." I sniffed and wiped a tear.

"A very special friend. He's here waiting to talk to you."

"Where?!" I spun around, peering into the darkness around me. "I don't see anyone."

"Close your eyes and I'll ask him to come out."

"What?!"

"Come on! Just close your eyes. He's a little shy."

I closed my eyes.

"Hey, no peeking!"

"I'm NOT!" I stopped peeking.

"Okay, now open them."

I opened my eyes and couldn't help but crack up laughing.

Then he did a really awful Mickey Mouse
impersonation in this silly high-pitched voice.
"Excuse me, I'm looking for a rat friend of mine.
Have you seen her around here?" He couldn't help
chuckling at his own stupid joke.

I played along.

"Actually, I haven't seen her. Sorry!"

"Well, I kinda like her. She's nice. And I just wanted to hang out with her some more. Can you tell her that? If you see her?"

"Sure!" I said, giggling uncontrollably. "If I see her, I'll tell her."

"Thanks."

"No prob!"

We both laughed so hard it hurt.

Brandon had a really wicked sense of humour. And nothing seemed to faze him at all.

I really liked that about him.

He took off the rat head and handed it to me.

"I think this thing belongs to you."

"Unfortunately, it does." I took it from him and shoved it under my arm.

"Can I ask you a really personal question?" he asked.

Brandon's mood suddenly seemed to have changed and he was gazing at me superserious.

I hesitated for a moment. I had no idea what he was going to ask me.

"Yeah. Sure."

"WHY does this thing smell so bad? WHEW!" He scrunched up his nose and narrowed his eyes like they were stinging from the odour.

We cracked up laughing again.

Brandon and I walked back to the building and Chloe and Zoey met us at the door.

They both looked a little upset and I just knew they were going to tell me off. I really deserved it.

"Nikki, why didn't you tell us when Brandon asked you to the dance?" Chloe said.

"Yeah. We could have helped out with the ballet party so you could have been at the dance the entire time!" Zoey added.

"We're your BFFs. I can't believe you didn't let us help you," Chloe said, looking at me kind of sadly.

I got a lump in my throat and felt like crying again. I couldn't believe they were actually upset because I hadn't let them help me.

"You're right. I should have told you both. I guess I didn't want to burden you with all my problems."

"Nikki, have you lost your mind?! That is just about the STUPIDEST thing I've ever heard you say!"

"Yeah! You must be suffering from oxygen

deprivation or something from wearing that rat head, because you are a talking like a CRAZY person!" Zoey added.

I could NOT believe they said that to me. Chloe and Zoey are the best friends EVER!!

They both came up to me and gave me a big hug.

"We forgive you. But if you EVER do something like this again, we'll personally force you to listen to a Jessica Simpson CD," Chloe said.

"For two whole hours!" Zoey added.

"I think the punishment is a little extreme. But I promise, I'll never do this again!" I giggled.

"By the way, those little girls really LOVE you!" Chloe gushed. "They said they want Mr Rat to come to their party next year too!"

"And guess what! Chloe has come up with the coolest

little keepsake for them to remember you by," Zoey said excitedly.

"Actually, I got the idea from my new book, *The Secret Life of a Teenage Party Planner*," Chloe explained, "but I'm going to need Brandon and Zoey to help out."

I thought it was a really cute and creative idea too. It took a lot of patience, but Brandon managed to take a very special picture with Chloe's new BlackBerry, while Zoey went around collecting e-mail addresses for each of the ballet girls' families.

Then, thanks to Chloe's superquick fingers, by the time everyone arrived home they all had a special little surprise waiting in their e-mail inboxes.

I'm sure the girls loved it.

Brandon is such an AWESOME photographer ☺!

Even though there were still technically ninety-two minutes left, everyone pretty much assumed the dance was over.

We were all just waiting around for the official announcement.

Principal Winston met with the chaperones for a few minutes and then walked over and whispered something to Violet.

Violet nodded to Principal Winston and picked up the microphone. "May I have your attention. I have an announcement to make on behalf of Principal Winston. He says he's aware that our dance is technically not over yet. However, he has asked that I inform you all that due to the unexpected disruption, effective immediately, we need to. . .

GET THIS PAR-TAY STARTED!!!"

Anyway, the second half of the Halloween dance was even more fun than the first half.

I almost freaked out when MacKenzie came up and told me the Halloween dance totally rocked. She said I had done a really great job as chairperson. Of course, she took partial credit for the success and insisted that I thank her publicly because none of it would have happened if she hadn't resigned.

Sometimes I think her severe lip gloss addiction has damaged her brain cells. That girl is so incredibly VAIN!

Then, when I asked MacKenzie if she had a date for the dance, she totally LIED about it.

She started bragging that her date was actually the lead singer of the band that was about to come onstage. And since he was going to be busy the rest of the night, she was hanging out with her BFF, Jessica. Whose date, BTW, was ALSO in the band.

I was really shocked to learn that two respected

CCP girls like MacKenzie and Jessica were using the old "My date's a band member!" trick.

How pathetic was THAT?!

Anyway, the lead singer, Theodore L. Swagmire III, was REALLY happy to hear THAT bit of news. Especially since he'd wanted to ask MacKenzie but was pretty sure she was going to say no.

When Brandon asked me to dance during a slow song, I thought I was going to DIE!

It was so TOTALLY romantic!!

OMG! My stomach had so many butterflies I thought I was going to have to grab MacKenzie's cute little $600 Dolce & Gabbana purse and use it as a barf bag.

But the biggest surprise of the night was that Brandon and I were voted Cutest Couple. . . by my BFFs, Chloe and Zoey!

Which was kind of weird because at this point we're just friends and still getting to know each other.

It's not like we're a "REAL" couple yet.

At least, I don't think so.

Unless HE thinks we are but I don't know it.

But I'm pretty sure he DOESN'T.

Unless I'm WRONG!

OMG!! What if I'm RIGHT?

What if he really likes me and thinks we're a couple?

Only, I don't know it YET!

Wait a minute. . .

I'd be the FIRST person to know it!

Wouldn't I?

DUH. . . !!

I'M SUCH A DORK ☺!!

belongs to: Lulu

Sird. 9yrs old born
2006 and birthday
31st Jan

Rachel Renée Russell is an attorney who prefers writing tween books to legal briefs. (Mainly because books are a lot more fun and pyjamas and bunny slippers aren't allowed in court.)

She has raised two daughters and lived to tell about it. Her hobbies include growing purple flowers and doing totally useless crafts (like, for example, making a microwave oven out of Popsicle sticks, glue and glitter). Rachel lives in northern Virginia with a spoiled pet Yorkie who terrorises her daily by climbing on top of a computer cabinet and pelting her with stuffed animals while she writes. And, yes, Rachel considers herself a total Dork.

Can't wait to find out what happens next?
Look out for the next instalment
of Nikki's diary...

Nikki's Road to Stardom checklist

☑ Diva showdown
☑ BFF feud
❓ Talented entourage to back up VIP (Very Important Pop Star)

**Nikki Maxwell's school is holding a talent competition and
she is determined to put her dorkish-ways behind her
and win. But then Nikki finds out that her arch-nemesis
McKenzie is entering the contest too and is planning to
steal all the limelight for herself. Can a dork like Nikki
take on the most popular girl in school and win?
Let the spotlight showdown commence!**

Go online for

Visit the Dork Diaries webpage

www. **DORK**diaries.com

for extra info on all the books
in the Dork Diaries series and the
author Rachel Renée Russell, as
well as a fab widget that lets
you create your very own Dork
cartoon!

Plus read Nikki's blog at

www. **DORK**diaries**blog**.com

where she spills extra gossip that
you won't find in the books, posts
competitions, videos and responds
to fans questions and queries.

more dorky fun!

And don't forget to log on to
http://series.simonandschuster.co.uk/dork-diaries
for exclusive video content, activity sheets,
news about the series and much more!